Weekly Reader Children's Book Club presents

SWIMMERS, TAKE YOUR MARKS!

SWIMMERS, TAKE YOUR MARKS!

by Nancy Veglahn

Illustrations by Richard Maccabe

Xerox Weekly Reader Family Books

XEROX

Text copyright © 1975 by Nancy Veglahn
Illustrations copyright © 1975 by Xerox Corporation

Publishing, Executive and Editorial Offices:
Xerox Weekly Reader Family Books
Middletown, Connecticut 06457

ISBN   0-88375-205-0

Library of Congress Catalogue Card Number: 74–17694

Weekly Reader Children's Book Club Edition

To the Brookings Swim Club

SWIMMERS, TAKE YOUR MARKS !

1

"It has to be down there somewhere. *Look!*" Clarity Moore brushed a lock of crinkly, brown hair out of her eyes, pushed her glasses up her nose and peered down through the trees. She could hear her brother Kip thrashing around below. In a moment he came scrambling up the mountain to stand beside her, red-faced and panting.

"The old railroad bed isn't where you thought, Clare. Either we're a long ways above it or we crossed it already."

"Well, you know what Dad told us—if we get lost we're just supposed to keep going down, and we'll wind up someplace where there's people. Let's eat our candy bars and then start back."

They sat under a tall ponderosa pine to eat and rest. It was so hot the chocolate bars had melted, and they had to lick most of the candy from their fingers.

"Great idea, going for a hike the first afternoon we've got some time off," Kip grumbled. "I'd rather be swimming."

"That motel pool has wall-to-wall tourists, and you know

it," Clarity told him. "You think I wanted to spend the afternoon charging around in the woods? If Dad hadn't told me to take my little brother for a walk . . ."

"It wasn't me that got us lost!" Kip was only eleven months younger than his ten-year-old sister. He was almost as tall as Clarity, and he hated it when she put on her "big sister" act.

"We're not all that lost, for crying out loud. We're right above the fabulous beauty of Silver Gulch. Granite peaks, mighty trees reaching toward the cloudless skies, cool mountain air, fish-filled streams bubbling through unspoiled meadows . . ."

"Oh, shut up!"

Both Kip and Clarity Moore had heard more than enough glowing descriptions of their new home since the decision had been made to move from Philadelphia to the Black Hills of South Dakota six months ago. It had seemed like a good idea, at first.

Their father, Leo Moore, had been an advertising executive with a large sporting goods manufacturing company. By the time he arrived at their home in the suburbs after a day at work, the rest of the family was busy with other activities. Everyone seemed to eat supper at a different time. Clarity, Kip and their older brother, Joe were pulled away from home by school projects and friends. Their mother, Peg Moore, was an artist. She had exhibits to plan, art club meetings to attend, and a night school course to keep up with in addition to her painting.

"We never see each other," Mr. Moore said one night when they all happened to be in the house at the same time.

"We never talk. Half the time I don't know what the rest of you are doing."

And it was true. They all agreed that there was something missing in their family life. "But what can we do about it?" Clarity asked.

That was when he'd showed them the advertisement he'd found in some magazine:

"For Sale: Silver Gulch Motel. A modern, forty-unit motel on the main tourist routes through the beautiful Black Hills of South Dakota. Filled to capacity throughout the season. Cable television, swimming pool. Contact Box 521, Granite, South Dakota."

The more they talked about it, the more Mr. Moore's enthusiasm caught on with the rest of the family. "Think of it," he said. "We could work together through the tourist season, the whole family. Then we'd have all winter to enjoy the outdoors, just put up a few off-season visitors or maybe hunters in the fall . . ."

"It would be a wonderful place to paint," Peg Moore said.

Kip looked admiringly at the picture of the motel in the magazine. "Our own swimming pool!"

"Yeah, that part would be neat." Sixteen-year-old Joe was on his high school swim team and had tried unsuccessfully to get a job as a lifeguard the summer before. "But South Dakota?"

"Maybe I could have a horse!" Clarity suggested.

One idea sparked another, and soon they shared a vision of themselves building a new life in the wilderness, a sort of modern Swiss Family Robinson. It was not until later that they had to face the prospect of breaking ties with friends, leaving the excitement and variety of the city, and moving to a totally strange place. By then Leo Moore had already bought the Silver Gulch Motel.

Clarity leaned back against the tree and sighed, remembering their first weeks in Silver Gulch. The motel was located in a valley (or "gulch" as they called it here) five miles outside the town of Granite. There was a little grocery store across the road, a ranch farther back in the hills, an old silver mine which was open as a tourist attraction, and a cluster of half a dozen homes which belonged to people who worked in Granite but preferred to live outside of town. It was quite a change from the Philadelphia suburb where she had lived all her life.

Not that she'd had time to think about being lonely. She had never dreamed it was possible to work so hard as they did that summer. Every morning forty rooms had to be cleaned, the beds changed, trash emptied, clean towels supplied. The telephone rang constantly, and even in the middle of the night people were pounding on the door looking for accommodations.

Even the motel pool meant more work than fun for the Moores. It was only fifteen yards long, and when the weather was good every inch was used by paying guests. Kip tried to swim when he had a few minutes free, but usually the only open space was at the bottom of the pool. He learned to swim very well under water that summer. Clarity tried it a few times and gave up. It was no fun to swim when you got an elbow in your eye every time you came up for air.

Now the season was almost over. Only half the rooms

had been filled the night before, so the cleaning had gone fast that morning. It was unseasonably hot for September. The pool was as crowded as ever, in spite of the empty rooms.

"Quit moping around," Leo Moore had told Clarity and Kip that afternoon after he'd refused for the third time to take them into town. "You still haven't explored Silver Gulch. Why don't you follow that old railroad bed up into the hills—maybe you'll find some old mines to look at, or you might see a deer. School starts next week, and then you won't have time for hiking."

"School," Clarity said, remembering. "We have to ride a *bus* to that ugly brown building in Granite . . ."

"Don't talk about it." Kip tossed a pebble down the mountainside. The lady who ran the store in Silver Gulch had a granddaughter Clarity's age, but Kip still hadn't met a single boy who would be in his grade at the Granite Elementary School. Besides, Clarity always made friends easily. She was already exchanging letters with a couple of girls who'd stayed at the motel that summer. Kip didn't like to just walk up to some kid and start talking.

"Well, we'd better get down before the rush starts." Clarity had almost said, "Before it gets dark," but she felt a little squeamish about the idea of being lost in the hills after sundown. There weren't any bears in the Black Hills, but it did get cold at night, and she'd once heard something about rattlesnakes.

"I'm going to climb that tree and see where we are," Kip said. "We might end up clear on the other side of the mountain."

Clarity watched her brother's thin, agile figure clambering up the pine tree. The branches were spaced far apart, and sometimes he had to dangle by his hands while his feet "walked" up the trunk. "Can't see yet," he called down to her. "I think I'll have a good view from the next branch."

She could see only his sneakers and the frayed cuffs of his jeans. Waiting, she noticed suddenly that this tree seemed grayer in color than those around it, and many of the branches were almost bare of needles. She tugged at a small twig, and it came off in her hand with a snap.

"Kip," Clarity yelled, "be careful! The tree looks kind of old and dry. Maybe you ought to get down . . ."

Later, she could not remember hearing the branch break, and she did not see Kip fall. She looked up suddenly and he was hanging there, upside down, one leg caught on a sort of stump that thrust out sharply from the base of the tree. His thin face was pale, and his dark blond hair hung straight down.

"Don't move!" Clarity told him, for he was still a long way above the ground. Somehow, she climbed up and lifted him until he could free his leg from the jagged stump that had broken his fall. That was when they saw the blood.

They both came close to falling more than once as they edged their way down. Clarity hung on grimly to the tree trunk with one hand and kept the other arm locked around Kip's waist. When they finally touched the ground, both her arms were shaking.

"It hurts," Kip said in a small voice, looking down at his blood-soaked jeans.

"A tourniquet—that'll help. I saw it in some TV show once. You tie something above the cut to stop the bleeding."

Clarity tried to sound as though she knew what she was doing as she peeled Kip's T-shirt over his head and tied it around his leg. She took one quick look at the red, gaping hole in his thigh and felt sick. But the bleeding did seem to slow down after she tied on the makeshift tourniquet. "Can you walk?" she asked.

"I think so. I saw the railroad bed just before I fell. It's that way."

Clarity half carried, half dragged her brother down in the direction he'd pointed out, along the path and finally down the last slope to the motel. It was like a nightmare. They did not sense time passing and had no feeling that they were making any progress until they stumbled across

the motel lawn and Peg Moore, standing at the window of the house, saw them coming.

Mrs. Moore drove him to the Granite Hospital emergency room. Clarity went along, still wearing the slacks and blouse that were stained with Kip's blood. The doctor on duty looked at Kip's leg for a few minutes, cleaned the wound, and told them that Kip would have to have immediate surgery.

The muscles in Kip's thigh had been badly torn by the tree branch. Even after the surgeon repaired the injury, he could not promise a complete recovery.

"It will take time to be sure," the doctor told the Moores when they talked with him the morning after Kip's operation. "The leg may be as good as new in a few months. Then again, he might always have some difficulty with it."

"You mean a limp?" Joe asked.

"That's possible, yes."

Leo Moore broke the gloomy silence. "When he gets home, what can we do to help get the leg working again?"

"Bring him in for physical therapy once a week for awhile. We'll show you some exercises you can encourage him to do at home. The main thing is not to let him favor that leg too much; see that he uses it."

Clarity thought of her brother's room, one wall solidly papered with posters and magazine pictures of football players. Kip's year moved from Little League baseball to touch football to midget basketball to baseball again, with an occasional moment of interest in Christmas or a trip somewhere. She wondered what he would do with his days if he couldn't play ball any more. And she knew Kip well enough to be sure he would not play if he couldn't keep up with the others.

Kip spent two weeks in the hospital and another week at home before he joined Clarity and the other students from Silver Gulch on the daily bus ride to Granite Elementary School.

Clarity was having her own problems by that time. For one thing, she talked funny. Nobody said much, but she could see it in the other kids' faces even when she said simple words like "water" or "rather." Of course their flat Midwestern pronunciation sounded all wrong to her—but they all talked alike and she was different.

On the afternoon of Kip's first day back in school, Clarity stood waiting for the bus with Melissa Lund. Melissa was a newcomer, too, but it didn't seem to bother her. She'd come to Silver Gulch in the middle of the summer and was to spend a year there with her grandmother while her parents, both medical doctors, were on a government health team somewhere in Asia.

"Didn't you hate to leave San Francisco and come 'way out here?" Clarity asked her as they jostled with the other kids to keep their place in line.

"Oh, sort of." Melissa hooked her long, jet-black hair behind her ears and smiled her crooked smile. "I'd been to Silver Gulch before, though, and I always liked to visit Grandma. Besides, I think it's fun to move around. I've already lived in six different towns."

"*I* don't think it's so much fun," Clarity said. "We've been here for four months, and you're the only girl I really know. And it's boring. There's nothing to do around here except work. Back home, there was always something going on . . ."

The bus lumbered up to the curb. As the riders pushed on, laughing and yelling, Clarity glanced around and realized that Kip was nowhere in sight. She and Melissa found a seat near the front. The she looked out the window and saw Kip.

Four other boys were ahead of him, running for the bus, calling to the driver to wait. Kip trailed far behind. He wasn't using crutches any more, and his limp didn't seem too bad in the mornings when he was rested. Now he was tired; the limp was very noticeable, and he knew it. He struggled miserably across the asphalt playground while the loaded bus waited for him.

"Clare, we've got to get old Kip to work on that leg." Clarity had not noticed her older brother, Joe, in the seat behind her until he leaned forward and spoke in her ear. "He isn't even doing his exercises any more."

"Isn't he?" Clarity was ashamed that she'd been so busy thinking about her own problems she had not noticed. "Well, I don't blame him. Who wants to spend half an hour lifting weights with their foot?"

"Right. Doing those exercises isn't any fun. We've got to get him started at something he loves to do, something that will build up those muscles. Swimming!"

"Swimming?" Clarity watched Kip climb stiffly up the steps at the front of the bus, holding tightly to the pole. "You know Dad drained the pool weeks ago. Anyway, it's too cold to swim now."

"Inside, dummy. That big, beautiful new Black Hills Sports Arena right here in Granite. Our gym class took a tour of it today, and you should see the pool—stainless steel, yet! Kip'll love it. Come in to town with me Saturday and we'll check on the hours."

2

"Wow, it's fantastic!" Clarity looked through the glass door to the T-shaped pool in the Black Hills Sports Arena. Yards of dazzling white tile bordered the clear, still water. The stainless steel bottom gleamed in the sunlight that filtered through from the tall windows. There was another, smaller pool just for diving, with two boards that looked like modernistic sculptures. The whole area was carpeted with some sort of spongy green stuff.

"Imagine this place in South Dakota," Joe said. "It's twice as good as anything I ever saw back East." He stood with a hand on the doorknob for a moment, as if he were about to walk into a cathedral. Clarity remembered how hard he'd worked to make the high school swimming team back "home," and she realized that he probably needed this almost as much as Kip. Maybe they could come every day, or at least several times a week.

They went into the pool area, and Clarity's glasses immediately fogged over in the steamy room. As she took them off to polish them, a man in some sort of sweatsuit came toward them. At least she thought it was a man in a sweatsuit. Without her glasses, Clarity was never sure what she saw. An old coat on a hook might become a werewolf, or a pile of shiny rocks could look like a fortune in quarters.

"Sorry, the pool's not open now."

Clarity wiped her glasses on the hem of her blouse and put them on again. The man had a plump, friendly face topped by thinning blonde hair. He held a ring of keys in one hand.

"Yeah, well, could you tell us when it will be?" Joe asked.

"Free swimming? Four to five today. Tuesdays, seven to nine."

They waited for him to go on, but he pushed open the door and held it for them to leave the pool area. In the hall, Joe said, "You mean that's all? Just those two times, when anybody can come here and swim?"

"Yes. I wish it could be more. Are you from Granite?" He'd obviously heard the Philadelphia accent in Joe's speech.

"We live at the Silver Gulch Motel," Clarity said. "But we go to school here."

"Maybe you could try out for the Granite Swim Team. They have practice hours every day. You see, that's why the pool isn't open for free swimming very often. We have classes, a synchronized swimming group, three teams that practice here . . . I'm Stanley Boyd, by the way. I'm in charge of the pool."

He smiled, and Clarity thought he certainly didn't look like the coaches in Joe's copies of *Sports Illustrated*. Maybe he was more like a janitor or something. Anyway, he was nice.

"Well, thanks," Joe said. "We'll be back this afternoon at four."

Clarity and Joe cornered Kip in the living room after lunch. He was reading a monster comic, his legs dangling over the arm of the sofa. Mr. Moore sat at the desk on the other side of the room, working on the motel books, shaking his dark head over a stack of bills. Mrs. Moore had set up her easel near the picture window, with an old sheet under it to protect the rug from paint.

"There's free swimming at that great new pool at the Arena this afternoon," Joe said to Kip. "Want to go?"

"Nah."

"Nine broken windows this summer," Leo Moore said. "Two TV sets had to be replaced, three dozen towels, seven blankets . . . no wonder we're not making any money!"

"I've got to send back to Philadelphia for more canvas and paint." Peg Moore stuck her brush behind her ear for a moment and daubed at the picture with a finger. "The art supplies in Granite are pretty limited."

Joe took Kip's comic and closed it up. "Come on, man, you're not going to get that leg working right until you get some exercise."

"I don't want to . . ."

"Good grief," Clarity said. "If you won't even *try* . . ."

"What it amounts to is, we're going to have to live on about a third of the money I was earning at Worldwide Sports Equipment," Mr. Moore said. "I'd hoped it would be better than half."

Mrs. Moore nodded absent-mindedly. "I ran out of my favorite red last week, and I just can't mix the right shades without it."

"Hey!" Clarity stood in the middle of the room, her hands on her hips. "Listen to us! Here we are, all crowded into this place together, all talking about something different. I thought we were coming out here to the wilderness so we could get to know each other or something."

"I know you well enough," Kip muttered.

"Go swimming with them, Kip," said Mr. Moore. "I can't works on the books in all this confusion. Besides, it'll be good for you. You do need the exercise."

The Sports Arena pool was as crowded as the motel pool on one of its worst days. Clarity lost all desire to swim in it when she saw the jumping, diving, kicking, writhing mass of kids in the water and all around the sides.

But when Kip and Joe came out of the boys' locker room, she grinned and waved to them from a spot on the side where there seemed to be a few feet of open water. She jumped in, took two strokes, and collided with a red-haired boy who swam on over her like an ocean liner going over a rowboat.

Clarity came up and grabbed the side. Kip and Joe were standing there, Kip with a towel draped over his bad leg.

"It's too crowded," he yelled over the din.

"No, come on, the water's really great." Clarity realized then that it was great, just warm enough without being like bathwater.

Joe dove over their heads into an open spot and swam across with smooth, powerful strokes. He was back in a moment, maneuvering through the other swimmers like a running back dodging would-be tacklers. "Come on, man, race you to the other side," he said.

Kip hesitated, then finally dropped the towel and jumped in. Clarity had a glimpse of the scar on his thigh before he hit the water. It was still an ugly red, but it didn't look all that bad. The important thing was for him to use the muscles in that leg again, build them up.

Joe swam slowly, watching Kip over his shoulder and leading the way through the hoards of swimmers. Kip struggled across, using mostly his arms as far as Clarity could tell. They rested at the other side awhile, and then swam back.

"Under water this time," Joe said before Kip could climb out, and they were off again.

Clarity pulled herself out and sat on the side, trying to pick out recognizable shapes from the blur of color and form. She saw a few familiar faces from school, but no one she knew very well. A number of the kids had identical green and gold suits. They seemed to be the better swimmers; she guessed it was some kind of uniform for the swim team.

"Your older brother is quite a freestyler."

"Hm? Oh, hi, Mr. Boyd. Yeah, Joe's a terrific swimmer." Clarity stood up and turned to speak to the man just as someone did a cannonball. Stanley Boyd brushed vaguely at his soaked shirt and stepped back a few paces.

"The younger boy—was he hurt recently?"

"He got caught in a tree in September. The leg isn't very strong yet. That's why we wanted to bring him swimming."

"Too bad. He won't get much exercise in this crowded pool. I know I suggested you all try out for the swim team, but the coach, Mrs. Marx, has about all the swimmers she can handle right now. I spoke to her just this afternoon. Tryouts were held several weeks ago, and they won't have any more until spring."

Clarity shrugged. That was the way everything seemed to be going in this place.

A moment later Kip limped by in the direction of the boys' locker room.

"You're not getting out already?" Clarity called to him.

"I'm tired!" He looked tired, and angry and discouraged, too. "There's no way to swim in this tank."

Joe stood beside Clarity and watched him go. "Guess I tried to push him too hard for the first time," he said. "Every time he got going he'd run into somebody. It'll be hard to talk him into coming back."

"We've got to. I don't think that limp of his is getting any better at all."

"Hey, I noticed a sort of schedule on the bulletin board out in the hall. Let's get dressed and look at it. Maybe there's another time that wouldn't be so crowded."

A few minutes later they stood in the hallway, wet hair plastered to their heads, studying the bulletin board. Kip lounged against the wall, resting his weak leg.

"7:30 a.m. to 8:30 a.m., Milton Minnows team practice," Joe read. "8:30 a.m. to 12:00 noon, classes. 1:30 p.m. to 3:30 p.m., Swim and Trim. 3:30 to 6:00 p.m., Granite Swim Team practice . . . No wonder the pool's so crowded for free swimming, with all this other stuff going on. Too bad we don't have a team or something."

"Yeah." Clarity stared at the bulletin board, as an idea swam to the surface of her mind like a lazy fish. "Yeah!

Joe, what if . . ." She noticed Mr. Boyd squelching up the hall in the wet sneakers he'd worn in the pool area. "Mr. Boyd?"

"Yes?"

"Um, this pool is supposed to be for all the people in this part of the Black Hills, right?"

"Well, yes, we try to serve everyone in the area. Teams and free swimming before and after school hours, adult lessons and other special classes during the day, various groups in the evenings—the pool is used almost all the time."

"Almost. But isn't there an hour or two, some time, that isn't scheduled yet?"

"Yes, but you see we can't afford to pay lifeguards and attendants for another free swimming hour, and they'd be at an awkward time of day anyway . . ."

"I wasn't going to ask about that." Clarity took a deep breath, glanced at Joe and Kip, and then looked back at Mr. Boyd. "We wondered if we could get a practice time for the Silver Gulch Swim Club."

Mr. Boyd regarded her blankly. "The Silver Gulch Swim Club? I've never heard of it."

"Well, it's new. We're just organizing it. But we could bring your own lifeguard. My brother Joe, here, is our coach, and he passed Senior Lifesaving a year ago.

Boyd turned to Joe, who rubbed a hand over his jaw and said nothing. At least he managed to seem fairly cool, as if he knew what Clarity was talking about.

"I can go back over the schedule," Mr. Boyd said at last, "and see if I can find a weekly time for you. How many members do you have?"

"Oh, a dozen or so," Clarity said quickly. "We thought we'd start small."

"A dozen." Mr. Boyd glanced at Kip, then back at the other two. "Why don't you give me your name and address? I'll see what I can do and get in touch with you." He took a notebook out of an inside pocket, found a pen and wrote down the information. Then he walked on down the hall and into the office near the pool doors.

"Well, Clarity Jean, you've really flipped out this time," Joe said in an exasperated tone. "The Silver Gulch Swim Club?"

"Why not? It's a way to have the pool all to ourselves, at least once a week."

"You promised him a dozen swimmers! Who're you going to bring, the dogs?"

Kip snickered, and the interest that had begun to show on his face died out. Joe noticed.

"Well," Joe said, "your friend Melissa would probably swim with us, wouldn't she? I know a couple of kids at the high school who ride the bus with us. Maybe we could dig up enough people—one thing about a swim team, you can use anybody from age six to eighteen or so."

"Sure." Clarity's words rushed together in her eagerness to convince them. "We can get every kid in Silver Gulch. Who wouldn't like a nice, free hour or two in that gorgeous pool?"

"Yeah, but we can't just play around," Joe warned. "I know enough about competitive swimming to know it's a lot of work, and Boyd will be checking on us . . ."

"Sure, sure," said Clarity, "we'll work."

Kip was looking at the bulletin board. "This one team's

called the Milton Minnows. What could we call ours, for a nickname? Let's see, the Starfish? Salmon?"

"Sardines!" Joe suggested, and the other two groaned.

"I know," said Kip. "The Salamanders!"

"That's not a fish," Clarity objected. "It's some kind of a lizard."

"We just studied 'em in science," Kip told her. "They can live either on land or in water, but they do swim. Anyway, the name sounds neat: The Silver Gulch Salamanders."

3

The letter came a week later, addressed to Joe:

Dear Mr. Moore:
  I have found a practice time for your Silver Gulch Swim Club. You may use the pool on Mondays, Wednesdays and Fridays from 12:00 noon to 1:00. We do require that you have a Red Cross certified lifeguard present at all times, and I presume you can bring at least a dozen or more swimmers. I will meet you here at the Sports Arena next Monday at noon.

Sincerely yours,
Stanley Boyd.

"OK, little sister," Joe said when Clarity had read the letter. "You're the one who got us into this mess with your great idea. Are you going to come up with a dozen kids by next Monday?"

"That'll be easy. There's you, Kip and me—three already. I know Melissa'll go, and you said you had a couple of friends you could ask . . ."

"That's six at the most. Who else?"

"Well . . . I think there's some kids who live on that farm down the road. And there's the two whose mother runs the drive-in out on the highway. Melissa knows them. And I saw a guy mowing the lawn of that green house last week. Didn't he play on your softball team last summer?"

"You don't even know their names, or whether they can swim or would want to be on a swim team. I think we'd better forget the whole thing, Clare."

"What about Kip's leg? It isn't getting any better."

Joe did not answer that. He stood up, stretched, and looked out the front window. Kip was sitting on the edge of the motel pool. The patched cracks on the bottom of the empty pool made it look old and forlorn. Clarity stood beside Joe for a moment at the window, then ran out the front door and across the lawn to the pool.

"I thought you were supposed to weed the flower beds this morning, goof-off," she yelled to Kip.

"I finished. Look who's talking—you haven't washed the windows on those last five units yet, have you?"

"Never mind that now." Clarity sat down beside Kip and tossed a pebble across the pool. "Guess what? Joe got a letter from that Mr. Boyd at the Sports Arena, and we've got a practice time for our swim club! Monday, Wednesday and Friday at noon."

"What about lunch?"

"Oh, we'll skip it those three days. We can eat our sack lunches on the bus going home. Lunch hours get pretty boring, anyway, when most of the kids go home to eat. Lucky thing the Arena's only two blocks from school."

"Yeah. You mean we really get to have that pool all to ourselves?"

"Right. Well, we have to dig up a few more members for the team. Mr. Boyd said we should have a dozen. What about those boys who ride the bus with us, the three who all look alike—what's their name, Kelly?"

"I guess so. They live at a resort back in the hills. I don't really know 'em—I sat with Mike on the bus a couple of times, and we talked about football."

"Why don't you call them now? Ask them to come and practice with us Monday."

Kip shook his head. "I can't just call and say, 'How'd you like to belong to this terrific swim team my sister dreamed up?' They'd think I was weird."

Clarity stood up and kicked at a pile of dead leaves. "You and Joe don't even want to try, for heaven's sake. Come on, we've got some time before lunch. Let's get Joe to drive us around and talk to some of these kids. I'll bet they'll be fighting to get on the swim team."

Mr. Moore had taken the family car to do some errands in Granite; that left the bus for transportation. A few weeks before, the Moores had bought a retired school bus at an auction sale. Mr. Moore thought it might be useful for bringing tourists in to the Silver Gulch Motel from the Granite airport, or even for providing tours back into the hills for motel guests. It would have to be repaired and painted first; that was to be Joe's job.

Joe had been tinkering with the bus ever since they had brought it home. He had it running fairly well now, but it still looked shabby and decrepit. A few scraps of yellow

paint clung to the outside among the dents and rust spots. Several of the windows were cracked and held together with ancient tape. Inside, half the seats were ripped, with dirty stuffing oozing out. The floor was warped. Near the back, one seat had collapsed like a carsick passenger.

Clarity and Kip found Joe rummaging in his tool box beside the bus. "How about taking us for a little ride in the old crate," Clarity suggested, "so we can see how it's running now?"

"A little ride? What've you got in mind?"

"Oh, I thought we might pick up Melissa and go see the kids on the farm, and the ones at the restaurant, and the Kelly boys—about the swim team."

"Look, Clare, I haven't got time . . ." Joe sighed and dropped the pliers from his hand into the tool box. "Oh, all right. I wanted to try that new drive shaft I put in anyway.

Clarity called Melissa while Joe got the engine going and

told her to meet them on the road. Melissa and her grand-mother lived in a house hidden in a stand of ponderosa pine at the end of a long, winding driveway opposite the Silver Gulch Motel. By the time they got there, Melissa was waiting.

It was the kind of fall morning that almost made Clarity glad she was not in the city this year. The lush, dark green mountains against the sky looked more like a technicolor movie than the real thing, and the air tasted like cold, crisp apples. As the bus chugged and bucked along the gravel road, Clarity told Melissa about the swim team.

"I don't know," Melissa said doubtfully, twisting a strand of black hair around her finger. "I can swim OK, but I'm not great or anything."

"That doesn't matter!" Clarity told her. "Just think, three days a week we'll have that gorgeous pool to ourselves. Besides, you'll learn to swim better. Joe'll teach you."

"Now, listen . . ." Joe said, dragging the big steering wheel of the bus around as they followed a sharp curve in the road. "I've never taught swimming, let alone coached a swim team."

"Oh, you'll love it," Clarity said. "You always did like to boss people around. Hey, there's the farm. Slow down. What'd you say the name of these kids is, Melissa?"

"O'Fallon. June's our age, and Dave's about nine, I think. He's kind of a pest."

"Never mind, we need everybody we can get."

A huge brown dog raced across the farmyard, barking furiously at the bus. "Hey," Clarity said nervously, "don't open the door till somebody comes after old Fang, there."

A sandy-haired boy who looked about Kip's age came

sauntering across the yard and called back the dog. Clarity recognized him as one of the kids who rode the school bus to Granite. Joe opened the door, and as they got out June O'Fallon came out of the house to join them. She was a short, stocky girl who wore her hair in one thick braid down her back.

"Hi, June," Melissa said. "Can you swim—you and your brother, there?"

"Swim? Well, sure. Why?"

Melissa explained, with frequent interruptions from Clarity. Even Kip spoke up once to describe the glories of the new pool at the Sports Arena. After that, Dave O'Fallon, who had been hurling pebbles over the top of the bus, began to look interested too.

"It does sound like fun," June admitted. "Are you sure you want the monster, too?"

"I can swim faster than you, any day," Dave told her.

"We have to get as many swimmers as possible," Clarity said, wishing they didn't need Dave O'Fallon. "Just go straight to the pool when you get out of class for lunch hour on Monday."

They drove farther back into the hills, up the winding Raspberry Gulch road to Buckhill Lodge. The Lodge was a sort of dude ranch and eating place, with log cabins around for tourists and a large central restaurant that sold food and souvenirs. It was owned and run by a family named Kelly.

Joe knew the oldest of the three Kelly boys, Ken, who was sixteen. Ken's brothers, thirteen-year-old Brad and eleven-year-old Mike, were doing some kind of leather work at a table in the yard when the bus drove in. Ken came out of the main building with a large piece of uncut leather a few moments later.

"Hi, what're you making?" Joe asked him.

"Stuff to sell next summer. Belts, little purses, that kind of thing. What's up?"

As Joe told them about the swim team, Clarity wondered idly at the resemblance among the three Kellys. They were all dark-skinned, with brown eyes that were almost black. Brad was stockier than the other two and wore braces on his teeth, but otherwise they looked like they'd been stamped out with the same cookie cutter. And here are we Moores, Clarity thought. Nobody would know we were related by looking at us. Not much alike inside *or* outside, I guess.

"Sure," Ken said in his quiet voice, "I've been wanting a chance to get in that pool. Sounds great, right?" His two brothers nodded and smiled like carbon copies.

On the way back to the motel, Clarity asked Joe to stop at the Quickburger to talk to Brian and Cheryl Stein. It was not quite so easy to convince them to try the swim team. They spent most of their time after school helping their mother run the drive-in, and they were not sure they wanted to commit themselves to three lunch hours a week at the Sports Arena.

"That's the only time I have to talk to my friends," Cheryl said. "We always have to come right back after school . . ."

"Yeah, and I usually play baseball or soccer after lunch," said Brian.

"Just come Monday and see how you like it," Clarity suggested.

The Steins finally agreed, but Clarity wondered how long

they would stay with the team. Back at the motel, Joe, Kip, Clarity and Melissa sat in the lawn chairs by the empty pool and counted their recruits.

"There's the four of us," Clarity began. "Three Kellys, two O'Fallons, two Steins—how many is that?"

"You'd better sign up for remedial math if you can't figure that out, Clare," said Joe. "Eleven."

"Well, you already talked to that friend from your summer softball team, Ted Beecher, didn't you? So that makes twelve. We're all set."

"I think we ought to have some extras," Kip said. "Those Stein kids didn't sound too interested. If we have just twelve, and somebody drops out . . ."

"Well, at least we're OK for Monday," Melissa said. "But Kip's right. We should find a few more, just in case."

Just then they noticed a small girl coming from the direction of the Quickburger, eating an ice cream cone. She had a freckled, pixie face and dark blonde hair. Patty Allison was her name, Clarity remembered, and she lived with her parents in a stucco house around the bend.

"How old do you have to be on a swim team?" Clarity asked Joe.

"There's no rule about it; you just have to be able to swim. They have races for kids 'eight and under.'"

Clarity was already strolling out to the road.

"Hi, there, Patty," she said heartily. "Do you know how to swim?"

"Not very well. I sink a lot."

"Would you like to learn?"

The Sports Arena pool was empty when they came out of

the locker rooms the following Monday noon, its mirror-like surface undisturbed by a single ripple. Sunshine leaked through the high windows and made bright spots on the green carpet around the pool. For a moment they all stood looking at it.

"Wow," said Mike Kelly softly.

The peace was shattered when Dave O'Fallon came hurtling across the room and cannonballed into the deep end with a shriek. The others followed, jumping, diving, or sliding cautiously into the warm water. When Clarity surfaced from her dive she saw only two people left on the side: Joe, and Patty Allison. She blinked the water out of her eyes and swam toward them.

"Hey," Joe yelled. "We can't just mess around. We're supposed to be practicing."

"Sure, we will," said Clarity, grabbing the side. "We have to get used to the pool, first. Come on, Patty, walk down to the shallow end and I'll show you how to dog-paddle. The water's great."

Joe seemed about to say something more; then he noticed Kip racing across the pool with two of the Kelly boys. Joe shrugged and dove in.

The hour sped by. Clarity and Melissa spent part of the time helping Patty and Cheryl Stein in the shallow end; then they took turns doing crazy jumps off the low board. The high school boys put younger boys on their shoulders and had wrestling matches that ended with everyone in a wild tangle underwater. Someone found a ball and started a game of "keep-away."

It was almost one o'clock when Clarity looked up and saw Stanley Boyd at the edge of the pool. Joe noticed him at the same time and climbed out quickly.

"We were just . . . ah . . . having some free time, Mr. Boyd. The team will really get down to work on Wednesday."

"Right. I see you have quite a group from Silver Gulch. It wouldn't matter to me you understand but there's such a demand to use the pool . . ."

"How was the swimming?" Peg Moore asked when they got home from school that afternoon. Mrs. Moore was at her easel again, putting the finishing touches on a watercolor of an old barn that stood behind their property.

"Great!" Clarity told her. "We had a blast. Hey, that's good, Mom—but doesn't it look a little too much like the real thing?"

"Too photographic? Maybe you're right . . ." She squinted critically at the painting and ran a hand through her unruly auburn curls. Peg Moore's naturally curly hair could never be coaxed into a conventional style for long, and she usually wore it in what she described as a "Scotch-Afro." "How about you, Kip?" she asked. "Did you have a good time at the pool?"

"Yeah, it was fun." Kip tossed his books onto the magazine table in the motel office and went on into the living room to turn on the television set. Clarity started to follow him when Joe said sharply, "Sure, everybody had all kinds of fun. Only it's not gonna last more than one or two more times. And that won't do Kip any good."

"Why, what happened?" Mrs. Moore laid down her brush and turned to look at Joe.

"Nothing," he said. "We all just fooled around for an

hour. I felt pretty stupid when Mr. Boyd came in, that's all. We told him we had a swim team."

"So next time we'll do some laps," Clarity told him. "What's the big deal?"

"You don't know a thing about competitive swimming, and neither does anybody else in that bunch. I don't know much, but I've been on a swim team before. We couldn't fool Mickey Mouse into thinking we've got one. The Silver Gulch Salamanders—ha!"

Joe slammed out the front door and strode across the yard to tinker with the bus.

"I don't know what he's so mad about," Clarity said.

"Maybe you'd better help Joe get that swim team organized," Mrs. Moore told her. "Regular workouts would help Kip a lot more than just playing around in the water. Either that, or drop the whole thing."

"OK, OK, on Wednesday we'll work like crazy. Is there anything to eat?"

Joe appeared at their next practice with a book he had borrowed from the library: *Coaching Competitive Swimming*. At the beginning of the hour he had everyone sit on the side of the pool in age groups.

Patty Allison sat alone at the shallow end, the only "eight and under" swimmer on the team. Her heart-shaped face was framed by a short, spiky haircut, and she slicked it down with one hand while Joe talked.

The next group was the largest, with four girls and two boys nine and ten years of age. June O'Fallon, Cheryl Stein, Clarity and Melissa crowded close together and as far as possible from Dave O'Fallon and Kip. Dave flicked water at the girls every time Joe looked away from them.

Brian Stein and Mike Kelly were the only two in the eleven and twelve-year-old category. They made a strange-looking pair, with Brian's pale, freckled face and slender build beside the husky, dark Mike.

Like Patty, Brad Kelly was the only one in his division. Brad listened quietly and made lazy circles in the water with his feet.

There were two new recruits in the fifteen-to-seventeen-year-old group, Russ and Julie Carpenter. They lived on a farm between Silver Gulch and Granite. Joe had met them at school and talked them into trying the swim team. Ted Beecher, Joe's tall, bony friend from the summer softball league, and Ken Kelly were the others in the oldest group.

"You'd race against kids in these age groups in a meet," Joe told them. "There are four basic strokes: freestyle, back stroke, breast stroke and butterfly. Today we're going to work on freestyle, since most of you already know how to do that . . ."

"Why work on it if we already know how?" Brian asked.

Dave O'Fallon splashed water in Brian's face, and the two of them traded splashes for a moment.

"Cut it out!" Joe yelled loudly enough to surprise them into stopping. "No horseplay while we're practicing. If we have a good workout we'll have a little free time once in awhile at the end. Now, here's how your freestyle should look."

Joe demonstrated the arm strokes, kick and breathing, first at the side of the pool and then in the water. It looked easy when he did it. Then he had them all stand up and told them to swim freestyle across the pool.

Halfway across, Clarity bumped into Melissa. They giggled and choked, but finally struggled back into the freestyle stroke and made it to the other side. Everyone else was there already except Cheryl Stein, who had given up and lapsed into a slow dog-paddle, and Patty Allison, wading across the shallow end.

"Oh, terrific," Joe told them. "At least you all got across the pool. Brad, you're supposed to turn your head to breathe when your arm comes up. Brian, you weren't kicking at all. As for you, Clare, you swim so crooked you go about twice as far as you need to."

"You know I can't see without my glasses."

"If you'd pull evenly with both arms you'd go straight. Everybody out, stand up and do it again."

After half an hour Joe started the older swimmers doing lengths of the pool instead of widths. Each time she dove from the block at the end of the pool, Clarity was sure she would never make it to the other wall. Somehow she dragged herself down the length and grabbed the edge, gasping for breath, only to hear Joe say over and over, "All right, get out and walk to the blocks and do it again."

"What's with your big brother?" Melissa whispered as they staggered around the pool to start yet another lap. "I thought this was supposed to be fun. He's turning into a slave driver!"

"I know. Must be that book—I think I'll return it for him."

Toward the end of the hour Joe borrowed a stopwatch from Mr. Boyd's office and timed each of them in swimming one length of the pool—twenty-five meters. Ken Kelly had the best time, eighteen seconds. Most of the older boys had times in the low twenties, and even Kip managed a twenty-nine. Clarity and Melissa both got twenty-sevens.

Joe wrote the results in a notebook. "We'll time you at

every practice for awhile," he told them, "and see if we can get some speed worked up. A fifty-year-old lady with arthritis could do better than most of you characters. OK, five minutes of free time."

"Thanks a lot," Mike Kelly muttered.

"Yeah," said Cheryl. "I don't even feel like messing around after all those laps."

"Who needs a swim team?" Brian asked Dave. "We could be playing soccer at lunch time."

Clarity was tired, too, and she didn't blame them. Joe didn't have to act like they were training for the Olympics or something. The swim team wouldn't last long if everybody quit.

Stanley Boyd came through the door. Seeing them sitting limply at the side of the pool, he said, "Well, looks like you've had a good workout today. Getting in shape for the meet, I suppose. I just came by to remind you to get an Amateur Athletic Union charter for your club, if you don't already have one, and of course an AAU card for each member . . ."

"Meet?" asked Joe. "What meet?"

"Why, the Black Hills Invitational, next month. It's the first big meet of the winter season, and it'll be right here at our new pool this year."

"Oh, I don't think we'll be ready for a meet that soon."

Mr. Boyd looked embarrassed. "I really think you'd better try," he said finally. "Some of the Board members have been questioning this practice time of yours, and if you don't enter the meet . . ."

Joe nodded. "We'll enter."

4

The Sports Arena pool looked different when Clarity and Melissa walked out of the crowded dressing room on the day of the meet. Bleachers had been set up along one side, and they were crowded with spectators. The eight lanes were marked by green floats strung like beads along dividers that stretched the length of the pool. Two ropes of bright-colored plastic flags hung above it, one a few yards from each end of the pool. Joe had told them that the flags were used by backstrokers to let them know when they were nearing the wall.

"I didn't know there'd be so many kids," Melissa said.

"Me neither," said Clarity. "Oh, well, we only have to swim against the ones our age. Why should they be better than us, just because they have those fancy team suits?" She wished she felt as confident as she sounded.

Joe had done what he could to get them ready for the meet. At the regular practice times he'd worked them all until they were ready to drop. Clarity had felt like a wet dishrag those afternoons after practice, especially since she didn't have a chance to eat lunch until she got on the bus to go home.

There had been a couple of swim team meetings at the motel after school, when Joe just read them things out of his book and explained the rules of competitive swimming. One unseasonably hot afternoon he even talked his father into filling the motel pool so they could practice strokes and dives. On another day he'd asked Mr. Boyd to connect the electric timer that was used at meets so they could hit the timer bars at the end of the pool to shut it off and automatically record their times. The results were then flashed on a lighted scoreboard on the wall.

Mr. Moore did the paper work necessary to get official status for the swim team. He had time on his hands now that the motel business was slowing down, and Clarity noticed him growing more and more interested as he listened to their talk about the meet. He sent for the Amateur Athletic Union charter and individual AAU cards for the members, and even talked of somehow raising money for team suits.

Still, a month was not much time to create a real swim team. Surprisingly, no one had quit in spite of all the extra work. Some of the better swimmers were excited about the ribbons and medals that would be awarded as prizes at the meet. Some just wanted to know what it would be like to compete.

And all of them noticed their times going down. In just four practices, Clarity cut five seconds from her time for twenty-five meters in freestyle. She began doing fifty meters, the distance she would swim in the meet. At first those two lengths looked impossible without a rest. But by the end of the second week she could do fifty meters without being any more winded than she'd been after twenty-five meters at first.

It was like that with all of them. Kip still couldn't keep up with the others in his age group, but his times improved steadily. Best of all, Clarity noticed that he could walk faster now, and his limp was not as bad as it had been.

Kip came around the bleachers now with their father. He wore a pair of sweatpants over his swimming suit. He was still self-conscious about his scarred leg, and Clarity hoped he would not be too uncomfortable swimming in front of all these people.

"Clare, look at the program. I'm in the first race, and you're in the second."

Clarity took the program, a thick blue-covered booklet. Inside, nine teams were listed. Silver Gulch had the smallest number of swimmers, and Granite had the most: fifty-six boys and girls would be wearing the green and gold suits of the Granite Swim Club.

Clarity turned to the second race, the "Girls 9–10 50 Meter Freestyle." The names of all the entrants were listed in the program, divided into four heats. Clarity saw that she was to swim in the eighth lane, in the first heat. Her "seed time," or best time for that distance, was listed as 51.2 seconds. Most of the girls in her heat had seed times in the forties. There was a girl from Granite in the fourth heat whose seed time was 38.10 seconds.

"Wendy Whalen," Clarity read. "I think she's that girl

with the big shoulders in Melissa's room. She looks like she's about thirteen. Boy, I'm glad I don't have to swim against her!"

"Your time will be matched against hers when they figure out the results," Kip reminded her.

"Yeah, but at least I won't look like such a nothing. These other kids in my heat are fast enough. Melissa and I'll be last."

"That's no way to talk," Mr. Moore said. "Get in there and try to win. You have as good a chance as anyone." Clarity recognized the gleam in her father's eye. He was a sports nut, and she remembered his wild cheering at a couple of Kip's little league baseball games back in Pennsylvania. It was nice to know that he'd be watching her compete for a change, along with the boys.

"Swimmers in the pool for warmups," the announcer said over the loudspeaker.

Immediately the smooth surface of the water was broken as one swimmer after another dove in. Melissa, Clarity, Kip and some of the others from Silver Gulch inched uncertainly toward the pool, wondering which lane they should use.

A girl in a green and gold team suit pushed through them, then turned back. "You're not supposed to be in here," she told them. "This is a meet. It's just for swim teams."

"We're on a swim team," Clarity shot back angrily, conscious that her flowered suit looked nothing like the sleek nylon team suits she saw all around.

"Oh, yeah? Which one?"

"Silver Gulch."

"Silver Gulch? *Silver Gulch?*" The girl turned away with a half-smothered giggle.

"That Wendy Whalen sure thinks she's great," Melissa said.

"So that's who she is." Clarity watched as Wendy Whalen climbed onto the sixth starting block. She looked bulky and rather awkward, standing on the block, but when she dove smoothly into the water and sped down the lane with powerful strokes Clarity could not help being impressed. Remembering Wendy's seed time in the program, Clarity told Melissa, "I'm afraid maybe she *is* great."

"Come on, you guys, get in the water." Joe came up behind them, looking tense and miserable.

The pool was so crowded by the time they got in that it was impossible to do any real practicing. All they could accomplish was to get wet and losen up their muscles a little. Then the announcer told them to clear the pool; it was time for the meet to begin.

Joe herded Clarity, Melissa, June, Dave and Kip to the "ready area," a card table in one corner of the room. There the meet officials checked the entry cards of those who would swim in the first races and gave each swimmer a slip of paper with his name, heat and lane.

Then Clarity handed her glasses to Joe and took her place on a bench beside the pool with the other girls who would swim in her event. The ten-and-under boys' freestyle event came first. Clarity watched, squinting to see as well as she could, as Kip and Dave got up on their starting blocks. Kip looked very pale, and in spite of his causal grin she was sure Dave was nervous too.

Stanley Boyd stood near the end of the pool with the

starting gun in his hand. His round face was pink and shiny in the muggy heat of the room. "Event Number One. Boys' ten-and-under fifty meter freestyle; two lengths of the pool. Judges and timers ready," he yelled. "Swimmers, take your marks . . ."

Dave O'Fallon went off his starting block, landing with a "splat" and splashing down the lane in a graceless freestyle until he became tangled in the false start rope which was lowered to stop him.

The crowd tittered as he climbed out and walked back to his block, and someone called out, "Yea, Silver Gulch!"

"That weirdo," Clarity moaned. "I wish the programs didn't tell where people are from. Why couldn't he wait for the gun?"

"Judges and timers ready," Mr. Boyd said again. "Swimmers, take your marks." The gun fired, and this time both Dave and Kip were slow diving off. By the time they surfaced, the other boys were a third of the way down the pool.

Clarity watched miserably as Kip fell farther and farther behind. When he reached the end of the pool and turned to swim back he was hardly using his legs at all, and his arms worked more slowly with every stroke. Dave was not much better, but he managed to beat Kip by several yards. When Kip finally touched the electric timer bar and dragged himself out, all the other swimmers were already out of the water and some were walking away.

The results of the first heat flashed on the scoreboard on the far wall. The winner of the heat ribbon had done his fifty meters in 41.87 seconds. Kip's last-place time was 54.19.

The other heats of the boys' event went by quickly, and

then the announcer called for the first heat of the girls' nine and ten-year-old fifty meter freestyle.

Clarity was to swim in lane eight, with Melissa beside her in lane seven and June on the other side of the pool in lane one. There were two girls from Granite, one from Milton and two from Lewisburg in the other lanes. Clarity climbed onto her block and looked down the pool. The deep end was a blur, impossibly far away.

She heard Mr. Boyd's command, "Swimmers, take your marks," and crouched with her toes curled over the end of the block and her arms extended, as Joe taught them. At least she was determined not to make a false start, like Dave. Finally the gun sounded and she pushed off.

Her drive felt all wrong. It was a near-bellyflop, and while it did not particularly hurt, she could imagine how it looked to the spectators. She came up and swallowed a mouthful of water the first time she took a breath.

After that the race was like one of those bad dreams where you try to run and get nowhere. The pool seemed to have stretched out to twice its normal size since their last practice. Clarity knew she was struggling too hard, fighting the water instead of using it to pull herself along, but she had to get it over with somehow. She touched the far end and pushed off, her arms feeling like limp spaghetti by the middle of the second lap. Twice she became tangled in the lane rope, for the more tired she became the harder it was to swim straight. At last she saw the end of the pool just a few feet away, and with what seemed to be her final ounce of energy she hit the electric timer bar.

Clarity relaxed, floating on her back and gasping like a fish out of water. She saw Melissa come splashing to the

finish in the next lane, and then June O'Fallon at the other
side of the pool. At least I wasn't last, Clarity thought as
she pulled herself out.

Joe was there, holding out her towel. "Not too bad,
Clare," he said. "Look at your time."

She squinted to see the scoreboard, her eyes stinging
with chlorine. She'd been fourth in her heat, with a time
of 47.24 seconds.

"Hey, that's four seconds better than my seed time," she
said.

"Yeah. If we can just teach you to swim straight, you
might make the Olympics."

"Never mind the compliments, just give me my glasses."

Suddenly cold, Clarity wrapped up in her towel and
found a spot near the end of the pool where she and
Melissa could sit and watch. The second and third heats
were called, and then the fourth and final heat of the race.

Three Granite swimmers were in that heat, with Wendy
Whalen towering over the others. When the gun sounded,
Wendy pushed off in a flat, shallow dive that carried her
a third of the length of the pool. She came up and stroked
down lane three, her arms working like extensions of a
powerful machine.

Wendy reached the deep end of the pool a length ahead
of her nearest rival. When she was almost to the wall, her
head ducked suddenly under the water and her body rolled
around as her legs pushed her off in the other direction.

"So that's a flip turn," Melissa said. "Too bad Joe didn't
have time to teach us how to do it."

"Yeah," Clarity agreed. "It sure looks faster than touch-
ing and turning around, like we do." Secretly she wondered

whether she would ever be able to master the tricky-looking turn. All the swimmers in this heat used it, and it seemed they had barely reached the end of the pool before they were on their way back.

Wendy won her heat and the race easily. On the last half of her final lap she only breathed once, and she hardly seemed winded when she climbed out. Her time went up on the scoreboard and the crowd cheered: 37.67 seconds. "New Record" flashed beside the number a moment later.

Clarity and Melissa grew bored as heat followed heat in the freestyle races. There were only a few Silver Gulch swimmers anyway, and they were nearly always in the slowest heats. The girls played gin rummy, bought popsickles at the concession stand, and talked for awhile with some members of another small town team, Lewisburg. Finally they wandered back to the bleachers and found a place to sit beside Mr. Moore.

It was time for the boys' fifteen to seventeen-year-old one hundred meter freestyle, and Joe was to swim in the last and "fast" heat. "Maybe old Joe can do something for Silver Gulch," Clarity said hopefully.

Joe looked good, and even did three perfect flip turns during the four laps of the race. There was not more than a stroke or two difference among the swimmers as they passed the halfway point of the last lap. Then Joe slowed just slightly, and finished—last.

"He could just as well have won that," Mr. Moore said.

"Gee, Dad, he's only had a few weeks to get in shape," Clarity reminded him. "That was the best heat, you know. He probably placed in the event."

"You're right. He's quite a swimmer, at that. And you

looked pretty fair, too, Clarity Jean. If you just wouldn't get tangled in those ropes . . ."

"I know, I know. I'd be ready for the Olympics."

Butterfly was next, and Clarity was the only girl from Silver Gulch entered in that event. Joe had spent most of the last week trying to teach her to swim butterfly, which he said was the most difficult of the four basic strokes. First she learned to do the dolphin kick, with both feet together. Then she worked on the overhead arm strokes and the eel-like movement of the body. Finally she tried to put it all together—and nearly drowned. She would try to breathe when her arms were driving down underwater, or forget to breathe at all, or lose the rhythm of her kick.

By the end of the week she thought she had the hang of it, but as she stood on the starting block and waited for the gun she was not so sure.

The first lap went fairly well. Clarity had no idea how fast she was going compared to the others, but at least she managed to do the butterfly as Joe had showed her. But on the way back it became harder and harder to lift her arms out of the water. Her lungs burned, and her legs felt as though they were about to fall off. She forgot about doing the stroke right and struggled just to get down the lane. When she finally hit the timer bar the other swimmers were out of the pool.

Joe was there again. "At least you finished," he said rather grimly. "I didn't know if you'd make it."

"I was rotten."

"It's a hard stroke, Clare. You haven't had time to learn it."

The other Silver Gulch swimmers did not fare much

better as the day dragged on. Melissa bettered her time in the backstroke by several seconds, and Mike Kelly was second in his heat of breast stroke. Ted Beecher placed sixth in the oldest boys' division of the hundred meter breast stroke. When the result sheets were posted on the wall, Joe's time was eighth for the freestyle. And that was it.

Clarity's name was at the bottom of the list in butterfly, and after her time were the letters DQ—disqualified. Joe told her she'd switched to the flutter kick toward the end of the race, and the lane judge had disqualified her for it.

Late in the afternoon the announcer gave team totals in the competition for the meet trophy. Granite was first, with two hundred thirty-seven points. Other Black Hills area teams followed, down to the Milton Minnows, with fifty-four; the Lewisburg Swim Club, twenty-seven; and the Silver Gulch Salamanders, four.

Clarity was sitting with her father again when the scores were read. "You'll do better next time," he said.

"Next time? What next time? I'm not going to make a fool of myself like this again!"

"Don't forget the reason for all this swim team business. I've noticed a lot of improvement in Kip's leg the last few weeks. By the way, where is Kip? The meet's almost over."

Clarity glanced around and realized that she had not seen her younger brother for hours. "Oh, he's probably playing cards some place," she said. "I'll go hunt him up."

She found him alone in a small recreational gymnasium down the hall from the pool, shooting baskets. He was alone.

"Where've you been all afternoon?" she asked him. "We

earned a grand total of four points in the meet."

"Wow, that's thrilling."

"Ted Beecher got sixth in breast, and Joe placed eighth in free."

"Good for them."

"So what are you growling about? You didn't do any worse than me, or Melissa, or Dave, or the other kids."

"You should have heard some of those guys from Granite in the locker room, laughing at us. The Silver Gulch Salamanders! We don't know how to turn, we make false starts, get caught in the ropes, DQ half the time, come in dead last . . ."

"All right! So what good does it do to come in here and sulk? I don't know about you, little brother, but I'm going to work twice as hard in practice, and the next meet we go to I'll show 'em all."

Clarity was really angry, and it didn't occur to her until she'd stalked dramatically out of the gym that she had been at the point of quitting before she talked to Kip.

When she got back to the pool, the meet was over and several hundred swimmers were milling around, collecting their things and getting ready to leave. Clarity dressed hurriedly and found Joe and the others in the hall with Mr. Boyd.

"We did the best we could," Joe was saying.

"I know that," Boyd told him. "And you have the makings of a good little swim team, but you see there's so much demand for the new pool, and some of the board members weren't too impressed with your performance today . . ."

"What's the matter?" Clarity asked.

"Granite wants our practice hours," Melissa told her.

"They have nearly a hundred swimmers, you see," said Mr. Boyd, "and they can't all use the pool at once, and you've only got a dozen or so."

Joe ran a hand over his still-damp hair and nodded. "I can see that," he said. "But we all got AAU cards and a charter and everything, and we're just getting started. How are we going to practice?"

"We could let you have the pool for an hour Monday through Friday at 6:00 a.m. I'm afraid that's the only possibility."

5

A touch of winter chilled the air that blew down the gulch. As the last stars faded, Kip shivered and fumbled with the snaps on his jeans jacket.

"Hurry up," Clarity told him. "Joe's got the bus going." Leaves had fallen from the elm street at the front of the motel yard. Kip and Clarity crunched through them and climbed into the bus. The motor chugged unevenly, and Joe raced it a few times to warm it up.

"It's the middle of the night," Clarity muttered. "We must be crazy. Kip, for heaven's sake comb your hair."

"What for? We're going swimming anyway."

"Because you look like a human porcupine, and I have to look at you all the way to Granite."

"So look the other direction."

"Cool it, you two," Joe said.

After that it was quiet as they bounced along the road. Joe stopped to pick up Melissa, the O'Fallons, the Kellys, the Steins, and Patty Allison, and still nobody said a word.

They slumped in their seats, still groggy from the night's sleep that never seemed quite long enough. Joe made his last stop at Ted Beecher's house, and then turned the bus onto the highway to Granite.

It was Monday, the third week of early-morning practice for the Silver Gulch swimmers. When Stanley Boyd had first told them that the only time they could practice in the Sports Arena pool was at six in the morning, Clarity had been sure that would be the end of the Salamanders. Even if they'd lived in Granite, it would have been hard to get everyone to the pool at that hour. To get them there from scattered homes five miles away seemed totally impossible.

But Joe was not ready to give up. He'd brought the team to the Black Hills Invitational meet in the old school bus, and on the way back to Silver Gulch he offered to pick them all up in it each morning and bring them to the pool.

"You just want to keep the team going because you won a ribbon," Dave O'Fallon said sourly, still smarting from his embarrassing false start in the first race.

"Face it," Ken Kelly said to Joe, "as a swim team, we just don't have it."

At first only Ted Beecher took Joe's side of the argument. "Practicing every day like that, we'd have a chance to get in as good a shape as any of the kids on those other teams," he pointed out.

"We'd have to go to school with our hair all wet and yucky looking," June O'Fallon said.

"Mom would make us go to bed right after supper if we had to get up that early," said Cheryl Stein.

Brad Kelly patted his plump stomach and made a face.

"First we had to go without lunch for swim practice; now you want us to skip breakfast. Don't you know that's not healthy?"

In the end it was Mr. Moore who swung them over to the idea of trying the early practices for a few weeks. He had come on the bus with them, and after listening to their ideas, he made a little speech about not giving up too easily. "So you didn't win a lot of ribbons and medals today," he said. "I was impressed with what you've learned in such a short time You don't seem like the sort of kids who'd quit so easily. With that daily practice you could come back and show those other teams a thing or two . . ."

"Never mind the old school spirit, Dad," Kip said. "I mean, this isn't exactly the locker room at half time. We bombed out, and now Joe wants us to drag out of bed in the middle of the night and kill ourselves swimming up and down that pool . . ."

"I was thinking," Leo Moore went on, "that I'd talk to the other parents and see what we could do about getting team suits for you."

"Now you're talking!" Clarity said, remembering the sleek, colorful suits the other swimmers at the meet had worn.

"A little bribery works, every time." Mike Kelly grinned.

"So why don't we try those early practices for awhile? At least they won't interfere with anything else we might be doing. Except sleeping, of course."

So the six o'clock workouts had begun. Every morning when the alarm went off, Clarity promised herself it was the last time she would get up at such a ridiculous hour. The ride to Granite was always silent, the passengers groggy and grouchy. The first few lengths of the pool seemed to take every ounce of energy Clarity had or would have for the rest of the day.

But gradually, the cool water and the exercise woke everyone up. By the time the hour was over they felt surprisingly good. Joe usually gave them a few minutes of free time at the end, and they had fun playing water polo or keepaway or just horsing around in the pool. Then they dressed and ate the "sack breakfasts" they brought—fruit, rolls or donuts, presweetened cereal.

As the weeks went by their muscles hardened and their skill improved. Even little Patty Allison could make a length of the pool with a fair-looking freestyle or backstroke. It took several sessions for most of them to master the flip turn, but after a few days of practice they discovered the turn was not as hard as it looked. Clarity learned to duck her head just about one arm-stroke from the wall, turn under the water and kick straight back with her legs to push off in the opposite direction.

The practices settled into a routine. First they all did ten lengths of the pool, freestyle, to warm up. Then they worked on their specialties for awhile, with backstrokers in two lanes, breaststrokers in two, butterfliers in one, and the other lanes for freestyle. Joe watched carefully and tried to help them correct the mistakes they'd made at the meet.

Clarity was still having trouble with the butterfly. She could do it well enough for a length or so, but as she grew tired her timing went off and her kick went wrong.

"You're fluttering again, Clare!" Joe yelled at her as she approached the end of her third fifty meters that morning. "Get those feet together!" When she pulled herself out and sat puffing on the side, Stanley Boyd was there with Joe. Mr. Boyd dropped in sometimes toward the end of their practice sessions, and he would occasionally help Joe with advice on some coaching problem.

"She just can't keep that dolphin kick going," Joe said.

"I get tired," Clarity told him, "and I forget about my feet. Maybe you better get somebody else to do butterfly. I could just swim freestyle . . ."

"Lots of swimmers have trouble with the kick in butterfly," Mr Boyd said. "I'll show you what the Granite team

does about it." He went to a storage closet behind the pool and came back carrying a stretchy, black band that looked like it had been cut from an old inner tube. He twisted it around Clarity's ankles so that they were held firmly together. "Now try it," he told her.

The first lap was not too bad, though the band felt strange around her ankles. On the way back it was horrible. Her feet seemed to weigh a ton, and her shoulders ached with the effort of dragging her body along. She knew her stroke must look all wrong. But when she finished, all Joe said was, "No flutter that time. Thanks, Mr. Boyd. We'll use it for awhile."

Clarity had to wear the band for a week, but when Joe finally let her try the 'fly without it she had no trouble keeping her feet together.

November brought colder weather and the first stinging bits of snow and sleet to the Black Hills. Melissa and Clarity left the Sports Arena one especially bitter morning after a hard workout and trudged the three blocks to their school, shivering in their ponchos.

"I think my hair's frozen," said Melissa as she put her books on her locker shelf and peered into the cracked mirror inside the door.

"It'll thaw," Clarity said. "At least it won't end up all fuzzy, like mine. One of these days I'm going to get this mess chopped off . . ."

"Hey, I heard you Silver Gulch kids are practicing before school now." Wendy Whalen strolled up from her locker and stopped to speak to them. "Isn't it pretty rough getting down here that early in the morning?"

Clarity looked at Wendy for a moment, trying to decide whether the other girl was being friendly or unpleasant.

She choked back a remark about how Granite had taken their lunchtime practice hour, and said simply, "It's not so bad."

"Not if you like crawling out of a warm bed at five o'clock in the morning to swim a couple of miles before breakfast," Melissa added. "And *breakfast*! You should see the junk we eat. What can you carry in a sack for breakfast? When I think of the fried eggs and bacon I used to have, with hot buttered toast . . ."

"You come down every day?" Wendy asked.

"All but Saturday and Sunday," Melissa told her.

"That's a lot of water time. You should be getting pretty good. But I wouldn't want to practice that early." Clarity thought she heard a note of respect in Wendy's voice.

Then two other girls came up, calling Wendy. Clarity remembered seeing them in green and gold suits at the meet. "Hey, Whale," one of them said, "we'd better get to class. What're you doing, giving advice to the Silver Gulch centipedes?"

"That's Salamanders," Clarity said, angered by the jeering tone.

"Oh, yeah, I forgot. You just swim like centipedes!"

Wendy laughed with the others, and they walked off together.

"Boy, I'd like to show those creeps they're not the only people in the world who can swim," Clarity growled. "They think they're so great. Centipedes!"

"Well, I don't think I'd want to be known as 'Whale,' either," said Melissa. "Come on, we'll be late."

As they turned the corner of the hall, Clarity saw Kip going up the stairs, one hand on the railing. His leg seemed to give him more trouble climbing stairs than at any other time. He was alone. Dave O'Fallon was the only boy she saw him with very often—and Dave was such a pill. Back in Philadelphia, Kip had always been in the middle of a gang of boys, running somewhere or other.

When they got home from school that day, Mr. Moore was outside patching the concrete around the motel pool. The sun had already dropped behind the mountain across the gulch, and he had the outside light on. Clarity realized that she never saw Silver Gulch in plain daylight any more except on weekends. They always left home long before sunrise; it was dusk by the time all the other swimmers had been dropped off.

Their father put his trowel down and walked over to meet the bus. It was still strange to see him puttering around in jeans and a khaki shirt after watching him come home from work for so many years in business suits.

"There's a package from Florida on the dining room table," he told them. They scrambled out of the bus and raced across the yard with delighted whoops.

Almost a month before, Mr. Moore had called a meeting of the swimmers and their parents at the motel. He'd made it a sort of party, and it had been fun to share potato chips and dip, soda pop for the kids and coffee for the adults, and just talk about the swim team. Then when everyone was feeling friendly and relaxed, he suggested that each family buy a team suit for its swimmer or swimmers. Joe had borrowed a catalog from Mr. Boyd. Together they picked a suit that no other team in the area was using, wrote down the measurements for each one, and got the order ready to send to the company in Florida.

"Which one's mine? Oh, let's try 'em on!" Clarity yelled, ripping open the surprisingly small package on the table.

"No, wait," said Joe. "I think we ought to leave them wrapped up until practice tomorrow morning. I'll look through the sizes and put on the names, so everybody gets the right one."

"Why can't we try ours now?" Kip asked.

"We're a team. I think we should wait."

"Can't I even call Melissa and tell her they're here?" asked Clarity.

"Let's make it a surprise," Joe said, and they could not talk him out of it.

Clarity complained about the delay, but the next morning she was secretly glad they had waited. The suits were bright red, with a gold stripe down each side. They were made of lightweight nylon, and they fit like a second skin. When the Salamanders came out of the locker rooms in their new suits, they were not the same assorted bunch of awkward beginning swimmers they had been before.

"Hey, look at us!" said Melissa. "A swim team!"

June O'Fallon ran her hands down the gold stripes on her sides. "This feels great. I'll bet I can take five seconds off my freestyle time in this suit."

"We'll find out," Joe told her. "We haven't had time trials for a week or so. Let's get the suits wet with a few laps and then I'll time you."

It may have been the suits, or the added week of practice, but almost all the times improved that day. Clarity's freestyle time went down to forty-one seconds, and her fifty meter butterfly time was fifty-two, a respectable time for that difficult stroke. Kip took eight seconds off his backstroke.

After the time trials, Joe had them all sit on the blocks or the floor at the shallow end of the pool. "We got an invitation to another meet," he told them. "It's two weeks from tomorrow, in Lewisburg. I think we ought to go."

"Will the bus make it that far?" asked Brad Kelly.

"Sure," said Joe, "why not? It's only sixty miles or so. We'll leave early, to be sure we have plenty of time."

"How early?" asked Cheryl.

"Warmups are at nine. I guess we'd better leave from the motel by seven. Bring a sack lunch or something. It'll probably be late when we get home."

Dave O'Fallon snatched his sister's towel and wound it around his head like a turban. "We swimming the same stuff as last time?" he asked, tossing the towel out of reach when June made a grab for it.

"Pretty much," Joe said, "except I want to have some relay teams. Quit messing around, O'Fallon, or you're not going at all."

"What relay teams?" Melissa asked.

"We could have freestyle teams in the ten-and-under girls, that'd be June, Cheryl, Melissa and Clare, and the fifteen-to-seventeen-year-old boys, Ken, Russ, Ted and me. The same two teams could swim in the medley relays, with each person swimming his own specialty."

"Neat," June said. "Too bad you don't get to be on a relay team, monster."

"Go breathe under water," Dave told her.

In addition to swimming workouts, they spent the next two weeks doing what they could to repair the bus. The whole team came to the motel several nights after school and worked on restuffing and patching the worn seats, taping the cracked windows and scrubbing out the inside. When they were through, it looked almost comfortable. And then, two days before the Lewisburg meet, it disappeared.

6

It was Patty Allison who told them the bus was missing. She got out of school before the others, and when they came to the corner where Joe had left the bus she was standing there wide-eyed.

"It's gone!" she wailed. "I bet one of those guys took it, like the ones who steal airplanes—you know, a jackrustler."

"You mean a highjacker, shrimp," Brad Kelly told her. "Hey, Joe, where's the bus?"

"Beats me!" Joe fished in his pocket and produced the keys. "If somebody stole it, they did it without these. Good grief, what am I going to tell Dad?"

At that moment, as if Joe's words had summoned him, Leo Moore drove around the corner in the "Silver Gulch Motel" station wagon. "Lose something?" he asked them, rolling down the car window with a smile, and Clarity knew it was all right.

Joe relaxed too. "OK, Pop," he said, "where's the bus?"

"Climb in and I'll tell you."

"All of us?"

"Sure, just squeeze in. I'm going to take you home today."

Somehow all twelve of them crammed themselves into the station wagon. Russ and Julie Carpenter always drove their own car, or there would never have been room for everyone. Clarity sat with Patty on her lap and the back door handle poking her in the side. As they drove onto the highway and out of Granite, Mr. Moore explained about the bus.

"We decided to paint it," he told them. "I was planning to get that done, anyway, before the next run of tourists. And with this trip of yours coming up Saturday—well, Peg and I came down this morning and I used the spare set of keys and brought it home. We spent the whole day working on it. I'd have put it back on the same spot and really surprised you, but it isn't dry yet."

"What color did you paint it?" Kip asked.

"Wait and see."

When the station wagon came around the turn to the motel, the bus stood out against the wooded mountainside like a misshapen fire engine. It was bright red, with the trim all done in gold and fancy gold lettering on the side: "Silver Gulch Salamanders."

"Just like out team suits!" yelled June.

"We won't have any trouble finding *that* in a parking lot," said Clarity, remembering the problems of big cities for a moment.

"But Dad," said Joe, "I thought it was going to be a motel bus. I mean it's neat, but with the swim team name on it . . ."

"That was Peg's idea. She did the lettering. It'll be easy

enough to paint out 'Salamanders' and write in 'Motel' if we want to. For the winter, why not an official swim team bus?"

"Yeah, why not?" Brian Stein agreed. "We may not be much in the water, but they'll sure notice us when we drive in!"

On the morning of the Lewisburg meet, the top of the bus was frosted with fresh snow. Big flakes drifted down out of the gray morning sky to the trees and meadows of Silver Gulch.

"It really *is* pretty out here, just like those gunky tourist ads said," Clarity remarked as the three of them came out of the house. "It looks like one of those little Swiss mountain scenes in a plastic bubble, the kind you shake and then all this little snowy stuff falls down . . ."

"Enjoy the scenery some other time," Joe said. "Come on, let's get the stuff on the bus and get going. We're already late. We've got to be there in time for warmups at nine."

"Warmups sound good, today," said Kip, shivering.

By the time they had picked up everyone and started on the road to Lewisburg, the snow was coming down harder and the wind was whipping it across the highway. Joe had to drive slowly on the winding road. The girls sang, and the boys played cards, and everyone tried not to notice how the bus rocked in the wind.

They were only a few miles from Lewisburg when the highway came around the side of a mountain and started down a long hill. By this time the snow was coming down much harder, and there was a soft coating of it on the road. When Joe touched the brakes lightly, the rear end of the bus swung out across the center line, then almost onto the shoulder, and then back into position.

He shifted into low gear and tried to hold the speed down that way, but near the bottom of the hill he had to brake the hurtling bus again. This time it swayed even more. Finally the bus skidded into the ditch like a huge toboggan and came to a surprisingly smooth stop at the foot of the hill.

There was a shocked silence on the bus, and then everyone was talking at once or giggling nervously. Clarity was glad the whole thing had happened so fast. She hadn't had time to be frightened, except for a second or two when she saw the trees beyond the road swing clear as the bus went off the edge.

Joe tried to drive back onto the highway, but the wheels slipped and spun in the soft snow and the bus settled back into the ditch. "Everybody out," he announced. "Get ready to push." He sounded confident and commanding, but Clarity noticed that his face was white and he was still gripping the wheel tightly.

A bitter wind chilled them when Joe opened the door and they scrambled out. The bigger boys got behind the bus, and the others ranged themselves along the sides.

Clarity grabbed the side of the bus and heaved with all her strength as Joe gunned the motor. The bus moved, hesitated with spinning wheels for a few seconds, and finally eased up over the edge and onto the highway.

As they crowded back toward the door, Clarity noticed Kip huddled in his jacket, shivering violently. "Hey, you OK?" she asked.

He nodded, but she could hear his teeth chattering.

"Dummy, you should have worn a warmer coat."

Kip ignored her criticism as he usually did, and she forgot about him when Melissa looked at her watch and yelled, "It's five after nine! We're missing warmups."

"Cant' be helped," Joe said. "We'll be ready in time for the start of the meet, anyway."

When they pulled into the Lewisburg High School parking lot, a few heads turned to look at the red bus with its gold lettering. They were too late to cause much of a sensation; most of the people attending the meet were already inside.

The dressing rooms were cold and drafty. When Clarity and Melissa opened the door to the noisy room, the heat of the pool area hit them with a whoosh. Clarity's glasses immediately fogged over.

"How many lanes are there?" she asked Melissa, rubbing at the glasses with a corner of her towel.

"Six. It's kind of a funny-looking old pool. Ugh, the water's a scummy green color. The starting blocks are plain old wood." Melissa was used to describing things for Clarity when she had to take her glasses off.

Joe came running up and grabbed them just as Clarity hooked the glasses back over her ears. "Come on," he said, "you two have to report to the ready area. You swim in a few minutes."

The meet began as they got their entry slips from the clerk. There were not as many teams here as there had been at the Black Hills invitational, but Melissa did remember some of the girls in her age group from the last meet.

"There's some kids from Granite," she whispered to

Melissa, "but I don't see Wendy Whalen."

"She isn't here. I asked her in school last week if she was coming to this, and she said no, it's mostly 'B' teams. Granite just brought their 'B' swimmers."

"In other words, Whalen is too good for this meet, huh? Well, OK, at least we should have a better chance today."

They watched the first event from their line of folding chairs along the side of the pool. It was the eight-and-under freestyle, Patty Allison's first competition. She looked very small when she first climbed onto her starting block, but she made a good dive and got off to a strong start.

Clarity jumped to her feet, screaming, "Come on, Patty, go!" These youngest swimmers only had to do one lap. Patty slowed down a bit toward the end, but so did the others, and she touched in second. Since there was only one heat in the eight-and-under division, that gave her a second place ribbon for her event. Melissa and Clarity ran to pull her out of the pool and congratulate her.

"Thanks," she puffed. "Where's my billfold? I want a candy bar now." She strolled calmly away.

"That kid is cool," Melissa said. "Come on, we'd better get back to our places."

Dave O'Fallon managed to restrain his dive until the starting gun went off, and he came in third in his heat. But Kip looked terrible. He hardly used his legs at all, and he trailed far behind the others. His time was almost as slow as those he'd been getting at practice weeks before.

Melissa, who swam freestyle in the heat before Clarity's, had trouble with her turn and did not do well enough to hope for a place in the event. "The water's as icky as it looks," she told Clarity afterwards. "I think I kicked a turtle down in the deep end. Watch where you're going, if you can."

Unable to see the lines on the bottom of the pool through the murky water, Clarity ran into the lane ropes twice and finished fourth in her heat.

There were only seven teams at the meet, and as the day moved on the Salamanders did surprisingly well. June placed in freestyle, Ted Beecher in breaststroke, Ken Kelly and Melissa in backstroke. Joe took two firsts, in butterfly and freestyle.

When Clarity got up on the block before the butterfly events for her age group, she looked over the other girls in the race. There were two from Granite, one from Lewisburg, and one from Milton. All of them were taller than she was, but at least there was no one as strong looking as Wendy Whalen.

Something felt strange when Clarity dove into the water, but she was too busy getting up speed to think what it was. She hurled herself in and out of the water like a porpoise, pretending the black band was still around her ankles so her feet would stay together. At least she didn't get tangled in the ropes this time. Somehow she seemed to be able to do the butterfly straight, even without being able to see the bottom. The stroke felt good today. When she touched in after her second lap, both Joe and Melissa were there.

"You won, Clare!" Melissa screamed. "First place!"

"Glasses," Joe kept shouting, "your glasses!"

Then Clarity knew what it was that had felt so strange during her dive. She'd been looking at the other girls in the race, and it hadn't occurred to her why she had been able to see them so clearly. She turned around and looked back along her lane.

She could not see the bottom of the pool through the green water, so she did a surface dive, came up, went down again farther along the lane. On her third try she saw the glasses looking up at her and snatched them just before she ran out of breath.

When she got back to the end of the pool a meet official was standing there. "You're supposed to be out so the next race can start," he said sternly.

"I'm sorry," she gasped. "I forgot and dove in with my glasses on."

Joe reached down and pulled her out of the pool.

"Did somebody say I won?" Clarity asked.

"You did, Clarity Jean Moore. First place, girls nine-and-ten-year-old butterfly, forty-six seconds."

"Whoopee!"

June, Melissa and Clarity sat along the side and nibbled graham crackers as the meet drew to a close. There never seemed to be a good time to eat a lunch at a swimming meet—it was always too close to the next race. So this time they had just brought a box of "munchies" to supplement the treats they bought at the refreshment stand.

"Team standings after forty-seven events," the announcer said late in the afternoon. "First place, Granite, with 172 points; second place, Lewisburg, 96 points; third, Milton 81 points; Fourth, Silver Gulch, 67 points . . ." Clarity did not hear the rest. She was on her feet, shrieking with the rest of the Salamanders. Fourth place! Their team was not a joke any more.

The relays were the last events in the meet. Clarity,

Melissa, Cheryl and June made up a freestyle relay team. They stayed almost even with the other teams during the first two laps, but Cheryl lost too much distance to the others for June to make up. They finished fifth, not good enough for ribbons in a relay, where only the first three teams placed.

Ted, Ken, Brad and Joe did better in the boys' fifteen-to-seventeen-year-old events, placing third. Then it was time for the medley relays. In these, each swimmer did one of the four basic strokes.

There were six teams entered in the girls' nine-and-ten-year-old medley relay. Silver Gulch had lane six. Melissa started out on the backstroke, and she stayed even with the girl from Granite all the way, with the other four trailing just slightly behind. Cheryl came next. Her breaststroke was better than her freestyle, and she did not lose too much water to the others. She touched in fourth, and Clarity dove.

It was always easier to swim in the first or last lane, because she could see the wall and keep her direction straighter than when she had to judge by the lane ropes or the lines on the bottom. The 'fly felt good today; she got the rhythm going without having to think about it. Coming along the last lap she started breathing only with every other arm stroke. She had no idea where the other swimmers were or whether she had caught up with the leaders. She was not thinking of anything at all except the movement of her own body through the water.

Clarity touched the wall, and June dove in over her head for the freestyle laps. Then Clarity saw the other freestylers diving off, one by one, and realized that somehow she had pulled ahead on the butterfly. She got out and turned to cheer with the others as June flipped her turn and raced back, still in front of the pack. The girl from Granite began to gain on her in the last lap, but June managed to hold on by breathing only with every fourth stroke. Silver Gulch finished first in the medley relay.

It was better than Clarity's first-place finish in the individual butterfly, or any other race of the day, because they'd done it together. The girls hugged each other, and the rest of the team crowded around, yelling and pounding their backs.

When the meet was over, Silver Gulch remained solidly in fourth place. They'd taken two ribbons in relays and nine others in the individual events, including three firsts. As they walked toward the dressing rooms, one of the girls from Lewisburg asked Clarity, "How long have you had that team at Silver Gulch?"

"Just a couple of months."

"You've got some good swimmers."

Joe heard, and just before they separated he said, "Don't let it go to your head, Clare. This is only a 'B' meet, you know. The really tough competition isn't here."

"I know, I know. But it was fun."

"Yeah. Where's Kip? I haven't seen him for a half hour or so."

"He and Dave were through before the relays. I think they got dressed after our medley race. They're probably outside."

It had stopped snowing, but there was still a cold wind blowing across the parking lot. Kip, Dave and Brian stood leaning against the bus when the others came out. None of them had won any ribbons at the meet, and though they had been excited about the strong finish of the Salamanders they could not really share the elation of those who had placed and earned points.

As they all crowded through the bus door, Dave scooped up a handful of slushy snow and thrust it down Kip's neck. In a moment they were on the ground, wrestling. Joe saw what had happened and jumped back out of the bus. He grabbed Dave, who was on top at the moment, and jerked him to his feet.

"O'Fallon, get on that bus and sit in the back," he commanded. "Alone!"

Kip started to get up, slipped on a bit of snow and winced as he caught his full weight on the bad leg. Clarity, sitting in one of the front seats, watched as he climbed the bus steps, slowly. "You sit alone, too," Joe told him. "And button up your jacket. You look half sick."

"I'm all right. Don't treat me like a baby."

They were all too tired to sing or even talk much on the way home. At least the roads had been sanded during the day, and they had no further trouble with the bus. It was dark by the time they got back to Silver Gulch.

Peg Moore had a huge pan of steaming chili waiting for them, and hot biscuits with honey-butter. Clarity and Joe ate like starving refugees as they told their parents about the meet, but Kip was quiet and not very hungry. After supper he began to cough. Mrs. Moore put a hand on his head and told him to go to bed at once. By morning his temperature was a hundred and five.

7

Kip was in bed for two weeks with a violent cold that developed into pneumonia. His leg was sore again, too, for he had strained one of the weak muscles when he fell down in the parking lot.

One Saturday morning the rest of the family was eating breakfast in the kitchen when the doctor called to report the results of Kip's latest tests.

"Then you think he can go back to school Monday?" Mrs. Moore asked. "You're sure he's ready? What about gym classes?"

"Ask when he can start swim team again," said Joe, but his mother was already thanking the doctor and closing the conversation. "He's not going back to those early swimming practices," she said after she hung up the telephone.

"Until when?" asked Clarity.

"Not at all, as far as I'm concerned. Kip's had a rough year, with the move, and his accident, and now this sickness. It wouldn't be a good idea to start missing sleep again,

72

getting up in the cold, swimming all that time and then coming out in the cold again . . ."

"But Mom," said Joe, "the whole swim team thing started because of Kip. It was doing him a lot of good. You saw how much better his leg was."

"Until this last trip. Then he got to fooling around and hurt it again. You know Kip. He'd never be satisfied just to practice and not go to the meets. Joe, it just doesn't seem to me it's worth all the effort. We can think of some easier sort of exercise for Kip."

"But if it's easier, it won't do as much good," Clarity pointed out. "Sure, swimming practice is hard work. That's why you get so strong doing it."

"Maybe so, but it's asking a lot of a nine-year-old who had surgery just a few months ago," Peg Moore insisted. "And the strain of all that competition . . ."

"Why doesn't somebody ask me what I want?" Kip asked. He was in the doorway in his bathrobe, slim and tired-looking but standing straight, with his chest out and his shoulders back. He's a pretty tough cookie, Clarity thought.

"OK," Mr. Moore said. "What do you want to do about swim team, Kip?"

"I want to go back to practice by Wednesday morning, and I want to stay on the team."

"Let him try it, Mom," Clarity suggested. "If he can't hack it, he can quit then."

"We'll ease him into workouts," said Joe. "Just a few laps at first."

"That fur-lined parka you just bought for Kip ought to keep him warm afterwards," Leo Moore added.

Mrs. Moore surrendered, but Clarity knew her mother

well enough to be sure that it was only temporary. "Just for a week or two, then we'll see," she said.

Kip was there the following Wednesday morning when Joe lined up the Salamanders along the side of the pool to talk about the state meet. "It's not until March," he said, "but with the Christmas vacation coming up soon there isn't really much practice time left. If we work hard between now and then, I think most of you can qualify for state."

"How tough is that?" asked Mike Kelly, stifling a yawn with his big hand.

"It's not easy. There's a qualifying time set for each event, and if you enter and don't make the time they can fine our team. Since the meet is right here in Granite this year, we can all watch it, anyway—but I'd rather have everybody swimming. Now, today let's work on your racing dives. They looked pretty sloppy at Lewisburg."

The water was a peculiar blue-green color that morning. As they swam, Clarity noticed that her eyes burned even more than usual. The chlorine in the water always irritated her eyes to some extent, but today it was especially bad.

Kip worked on the dives and did a few laps, but Joe had him put on his sweatsuit and sit at the side of the pool for more than half the hour. He didn't argue about it.

As they were getting out of the pool Mr. Boyd appeared and asked them how the water was.

"About the right temperature," Joe told him. "But I think maybe the chlorine's a bit strong."

Mr. Boyd studied the pool with a worried little frown between his eyebrows. "The color's strange, don't you think? I don't know what happened. We're trying some new chemicals and a process for changing the water that

the manufacturer suggested. One of the pumps isn't working right, either. You'd think a new pool like this . . ." He
wandered on down along the side, mumbling to himself
and peering down at the water

By the time she got to social studies class that day,
Clarity's eyes were so sore she could not look at her book
without squinting painfully after a few minutes. Melissa
and June's eyes looked red too.

Later that morning she passed Dave O'Fallon in the hall,
and noticed that he was scratching fiercely at his left arm.
She did not think too much about that until she saw Melissa
scratching her shoulder. Then, as they waited in line by
the drinking fountain, Clarity felt a terrible itching sensation at the back of her neck.

"Hey, Meliss," she said, "I feel like I just got bit on the
neck by a starving mosquito. Are you itchy too?"

"Yeah; for awhile it was my shoulder but now my leg
itches."

"I saw Dave scratching his arm awhile ago. Here comes
Kip, let's ask him . . . Ooops, I guess we don't need to ask."

Kip was scratching his chest. "What are you staring at?"
he asked them

"You," said Clarity. "Either we all walked through a patch
of poison ivy on the way to school this morning or there was
something wrong with the water at the pool."

"What?"

"Look around. Our eyes are red, we're all itching—hey,
Brian!"

Brian Stein pushed through the crowd in the hall, a
grumpy look on his freckled face. There was a bright red

patch on his right hand. "What's going on?" he asked. "Old MacDougal'll kill me if I'm late to class again."

"What's wrong with your hand?" Clarity asked him. "Have you been scratching it?"

"You got me over here to find out if I've been scratching my hand?"

"Well, have you?"

"Yeah. Is it against the rules or something?"

"Clare thinks there was something wrong with the water at the pool this morning," Kip told him.

The bell rang just then, and they all had to run for their rooms. The last hour of the morning crawled by like an hour in the dentist's chair. Clarity read the same sentence over and over as "the itch" moved from her neck to the middle of her back, then around her waist.

By the time they lined up for hot lunch it was easy to pick out the Silver Gulch Salamanders, if you knew what to look for. It was like some sort of secret society, only instead of a password or sign of recognition or badge the members could be known by their red eyes, scaly skin and frantic scratching.

Wendy Whalen and a half dozen other members of the Granite swim team were just ahead of Clarity and Melissa in the lunch line. "Hey, are you Silver Gulch Centipedes getting all ready for the state meet?" asked a girl with pale blonde hair and braces.

"Sure, we're working on it," Clarity said, ignoring the gibe.

"Think any of you can qualify?" asked Wendy.

Clarity concentrated on not scratching her elbow. "We're all going to qualify; or most of us anyway."

"Oooo, we'll have to be careful," the blonde girl said

nastily. "What would we do if all six of them came?"

"Fourteen," Melissa corrected her.

"Have you two got fleas or something?" asked another of the Granite girls.

Clarity and Melissa stopped scratching. As the others got their trays and walked off together, Melissa said, "Shouldn't we tell them about the pool?"

"We should tell Mr. Boyd, I guess," Clarity said. "They have practice after school today, don't they? Wouldn't it be too bad if we didn't get over there until they'd already been swimming awhile?"

"Sounds like kind of a mean trick."

"Why should we break our necks to warn them about the water?" Clarity picked up her tray. "Ugh, cooked carrots. No, I think it might be sort of funny to see the whole Granite swim team walking around with 'the itch' tomorrow. Silver Gulch Centipedes! Let 'em find out about the water themselves!"

They endured the afternoon somehow. Melissa was late in coming to her locker after school, and as Clarity waited for her she noticed Wendy Whalen striding down the hall. Wendy towered over everyone else, and Clarity remembered how she had looked in the water at the last meet.

She's a beautiful swimmer, Clarity told herself. So maybe you're a little jealous?

"Hey, Wendy," she called. "Look at this." She held out her red, scaly arms. "I think the Salamanders discovered a new disease this morning: swimmers' leprosy."

"You got that way from swimming?"

"Yep. There was something wrong with the water in the pool today. We're all itching like mad. You better tell your coach to call off practice."

"Well, I will," Wendy said. "Say, thanks." She smiled, and Clarity remembered with guilt how close she had come to not warning the Granite swimmers.

Stanley Boyd was not in his office when Clarity and Melissa got there. They found him beside the pool, measuring out a little vial of water.

"Be with you in a minute, girls," he said. "I've got to have this tested. It just doesn't look right today. I had a call from a member of our Swim 'n Trim class, said her skin was breaking out. It's probably nothing, but . . ."

Clarity and Melissa held out their arms wordlessly as he turned to them.

"Oh, no! Does it—itch?"

"Like mad," said Clarity.

Mrs. Marx, the Granite coach, came into the room with a clipboard in one hand and a towel in the other. She was a bony woman with thin, reddish hair and jeweled glasses that went up at the corners like Batman's mask. "What's the problem?" she asked Mr. Boyd.

"Well, we may have a chemical imbalance or a micro-organism in the water . . ."

"Can we practice or not? Whalen says she heard there's some kind of itch people are getting from the pool."

"Yes, it looks that way. You'd better call off practice."

"When will you have it taken care of?"

"I'm afraid we'll have to drain the pool. I just can't say right now. It might be several days."

"Too long," Mrs. Marx snapped. "We can't miss that much practice. Get on it." She walked away, her clogs slapping loudly on the damp carpet.

"She doesn't waste words, does she?" said Clarity.

Mr. Boyd smiled and shrugged. "Oh, Marx is all right.

She just talks in shorthand. Too many years of yelling at swimmers, I guess. But she will be disgusted if we don't get this cleared up soon. I'd better get this sample to the chemist right away."

They lost a week of practice while Stanley Boyd got the water purified and the pool drained and filled again. "The itch," which they learned had been caused by a mistake in the mixing of some chemical used to treat the water, did not last long. Soda baths and lotions took care of the worst of it, and within a day or two all the Salamanders were back to normal.

"It's going to seem funny to have Christmas with just us this year," Clarity said as she helped her mother unpack the decorations on the first day of vacation.

"Yes, it'll be different without all the relatives." Mrs. Moore unrolled a banner she had made the year before and hung it on the wall. It said simply, "Alleluia!", but the bright colors made it more of a shout.

Kip and Joe had spread newspapers on the kitchen floor. They were sawing pine cones in half to make a wreath for the front door. "Too bad we couldn't go back to Philadelphia for Christmas," Kip said. "When are we going to buy the tree?"

"We're not exactly going to buy it," Mrs. Moore told him. "Your dad found out that there's an area up in the hills where we can go and cut down our own Christmas tree. We just have to pay a small fee and get a tag; then we can go and pick it out ourselves."

"You mean we can go cut down a tree right out in the woods? Neat!" Kip said. "When do we do it?"

"How about now?" Mr. Moore came through the front

door and motioned to them. He looked like a real woods-man, with his red plaid jacket and an axe in one hand. "Come on, I've got the tag for the tree. We want to get up there before dark."

They left the Christmas decorations where they were, put on their coats and boots and piled into the bus. The afternoon was cold, but clear and sunny. It had snowed the day before, and all the trees and jutting granite rocks were frosted with glistening white. Joe brought his battered guitar along. He used it to pick out Christmas carols, and they sang with the guitar as Mr. Moore drove the bus along the winding hill roads: "I Saw Three Ships," and "The Twelve Days of Christmas," and "God Rest Ye, Merry Gentlemen."

The area where the trees could be cut down was high in the hills. Mr. Moore parked the bus just off the road, and they began looking for the perfect Christmas tree. Clarity found one she liked, but Joe noticed a thin spot on one side. Mrs. Moore's choice had a crooked trunk, and Kip picked one that was too tall to go in the bus.

Finally Leo Moore, Clarity and Kip all spotted the tree at the same time: a fat pine with tiny cones all over it.

"Look, it's already decorated!" Clarity said.

They all took turns with the axe, scrambling to get out of the way when the tree fell in an unexpected direction. Together they carried it down to the bus, dusting their coats with the powdered sugar snow in the process.

That night Joe and Mr. Moore set it up in the living room beside the front window. "It really doesn't need much more in the way of decorations," Peg Moore said. "Just the lights."

"Why don't we make it an old fashioned tree?" Clarity

suggested. "I've been reading about 'em in school. Strings of popcorn and cranberries, and then put it out to feed the birds after Christmas."

Mrs. Moore and Clarity spent the evening stringing popcorn and cranberries while the boys finished their pine-cone wreath and Mr. Moore put the lights on the tree. They ate the rest of the popcorn and drank hot cocoa, and then Joe got his guitar to accompany them in more singing. Even Kip joined in, though he usually considered family sing-alongs too corny for him. It was nearly midnight when they turned off all the lights except those on the tree and sang, "O Christmas Tree."

Later, Clarity lay on her side in bed and looked out the window at the dark hills against the moonlit sky. It seemed almost as if tonight had been Christmas, though all the presents were still hidden away in their wrappings. Her legs were tired from tramping through the woods, and her fingers stung with needle pricks she'd gotten while stringing popcorn and cranberries. No particular part of the day seemed like such a big deal, but there was a special feeling in the winter night. She was too tired to think why.

When the swim team practices began after Christmas vacation, Joe worked them without mercy. Brian Stein, who always had the best grades in math class at school, figured out that they averaged more than three thousand yards of swimming every morning. Often they started with twenty lengths of the pool just to warm up; then they worked on their individual specialty strokes.

Clarity swam in a lane with the other butterfliers, Brad Kelly and Brian. She could go almost as fast as Brian, and sometimes she even beat him, but thirteen-year-old Brad left them both behind. Once in awhile Joe got in and practiced with them, especially if Mr. Boyd came into give a few minutes of help to the breaststrokers and backstrokers. Stanley Boyd had been a college swimming coach before he became manager of the Sports Arena. He didn't look like a swimmer, but then Clarity had never seen him in the pool.

Kip was able to keep up quite well now. His backstroke looked especially good, and he didn't tire after a few laps as he had earlier in the year.

One February morning Joe planned to time all of them and see who could qualify for the state meet. Outside the motel the thermometer registered twenty-two below zero. He started the bus early to let it warm up. The snow made a peculiar squeaking sound as they ran across the lawn to get in, and the air was so cold it hurt to breathe.

Clarity still felt half asleep when she came out of the dressing room at the Sports Arena, and for a moment she thought she'd forgotten to bring her glasses. Her hand went up automatically and felt the bow under her hair—and yet she couldn't see.

The swimming pool room was shrouded in fog. The thick, gray stuff hung over the water like a lost cloud.

"What's going on?" Dave O'Fallon yelled from somewhere across the room. "Did somebody light a fire in here?"

"It's just that super-cold air," Clarity heard Mr. Boyd say behind her. "On a morning this cold, that warm water can fog the room up like a bathroom when you take a hot shower. I don't think it will last too long."

"OK," Joe said. "It's not that bad. Up on the blocks."

"If we can find 'em," someone said.

It was weird, swimming up and down the pool through the fog. "I can't see when to flip my turn," Melissa complained during a short break.

"Yeah," June said, "and I keep bumping into people. I got clear over in the next lane a few minutes ago."

"Now you know how I feel all the time without my glasses," Clarity told them.

By the time they were through with warmups, the fog had cleared. Joe sat in the lifeguard's chair with a stopwatch he'd borrowed from the Arena office and a notebook to write down each swimmer's times in the different strokes.

After the time trials, he had all the Salamanders sit along the side of the pool to hear the results. Clarity studied his face, trying to guess how they'd done. She had never thought of Joe as a person who showed his feelings, but lately she'd been with her older brother so much that she had begun to recognize certain telltale expressions. She saw the slight crinkling at the corners of his eyes now, and guessed that he was pleased.

"Silver Gulch will have ten swimmers entered in the state meet," he told them. When the cheering stopped he explained that only Patty Allison, Mike and Brad Kelly and Julie Carpenter had failed to qualify in some event. The Kelly boys had both been sick during the past few weeks, and Julie was so involved in school activities that she didn't get to practice very often.

Clarity would swim in the freestyle, butterfly and the medley relay. Her freestyle time was not too impressive, but at least she could enter, and her butterfly time was well under the limit.

Best of all, Kip had qualified in both backstroke and freestyle.

8

The card table was crowded with food: sweet rolls with creamy frosting, huge glazed donuts, bowls of orange sections, pitchers of fruit juice, mugs of foaming hot chocolate. On the wall behind the table hung a red-and-gold banner lettered, "Good Luck Salamanders."

It was the morning of their last practice before the state meet. Joe had not worked the team quite as hard as usual, in order to save their energy for the coming two days. He let them get out of the pool fifteen minutes early, and when they came out of the locker rooms they saw why.

Peg and Leo Moore were there, along with Mrs. Kelly, the O'Fallons, Mrs. Stein and Melissa's grandmother. They'd all helped to bring the surprise breakfast.

There was an awkward moment when none of the swimmers knew quite what to say, but Dave O'Fallon broke the mood of shyness by reaching for a donut. "Great idea," he bellowed. "I'm starved!"

"This tastes fantastic," Clarity said after her second roll.

"You ought to do it every day." She saw the look on her mother's face, and added hastily, "Well, once a week anyway."

"We won't have any more early morning practices this year," Joe reminded her. "The winter season's over after the state meet, and this summer we should be able to get different hours."

"This summer?" Mr. Moore asked. "Wait a minute, Joe, don't forget the motel. You remember how busy we were last year during the tourist season. I don't see how you could practice every day and take off for weekend meets this summer."

"Our boys will be working at the Lodge," Mr. Kelly said.

Mrs. Stein agreed. "I'll need Brian and Cheryl at the drive-in."

"All right," Joe said, "looks like this is it until next fall anyway. We're going to let everybody know we've got a swim team."

Clarity had belonged to a girl scout troop in Philadelphia. On one overnight campout at a park, more girls had decided to go along than had been expected. Eighteen of them had tried to share one medium-sized tent.

The scene in the locker room at the Sports Arena the next morning reminded her of that overnight. Girls from all over South Dakota were jammed into the room, along with heaped towels, clothes, combs and brushes, bags of potato chips, candy bars, portable radios, blankets, sleeping bags, playing cards and games, comic books, and at least fifty zippered gym bags.

Clarity and Melissa huddled on a bench at one corner of

the room. They already had their suits on and were studying the program for the weekend.

Melissa counted sixteen teams taking part in the meet. "We aren't even the smallest," she said. "Look, here's one with only three swimmers who qualified, and we've got ten!"

"What's my seed time for the butterfly?" Clarity asked her.

"Wait a minute, I want to check my backstroke event. Hey, I'm in the fast heat; there's only four kids that have better times than me." Melissa flipped the pages to the listing for butterfly. "And you look good, too, Clare. You're in the fast heat, see?"

"Not as good as Whalen, though. Thirty-eight seconds, they've got her down for. You think she can really do that? Joe put forty-three for me, and I've only made that a couple of times."

"That's still better than three others in the heat. You ought to place."

"Yeah, if I don't run into the ropes or something." Clarity looked around the locker room. "This place is a mess; I can't leave my glasses in here. Besides, I want to see the other events. I'll give 'em to Joe or Dad, just before I swim."

"Just don't dive in with them on your face, like you did at Lewisburg. Come on, I hear the announcer out there. It must be time for warmups."

The pool area looked even more chaotic than the locker room. One whole side of the room was taken up with bleachers. Adults who could not find a place to sit there had set up folding chairs. Most of the swimmers sat on the floor with their teams in a tangle of towels, sweatsuits and other belongings. Benches along the other side of the pool were reserved for swimmers waiting to be called for an approaching event. The "ready area," at the back of the big room, swarmed with mass confusion as swimmers in sixteen different team suits crowded around a table to get their entry cards for the first events.

Parents of Granite swimmers had set up a refreshment stand near the door to the hall. "Good way to make money for the team," Clarity said as she bought a snow cone. "Sure you don't want one?"

"No, I have to swim in a few minutes," Melissa said. "Ugh, I don't see how you can eat that at nine o'clock in the morning. Aren't you nervous?"

"Sure. I get hungry when I'm nervous." Clarity glanced at the list of food and the prices. "I've got to make a dollar last all day. Boy, it's too bad we can't have a meet. We could really make money. Maybe even get neat sweatshirts like the Granite kids have . . ."

"Come on, I've got to get my entry card."

Backstroke came first at this meet. Melissa went to wait for her race, and Clarity squeezed into a tiny spot by the pool where the other Salamanders were watching the slower heats of the boys ten-and-under backstroke. She nibbled at the snow cone and waited for Kip to be called.

He was in one of the faster heats, and his seed time was only a few seconds off those of some of the top swimmers in the event. Joe had been working him especially hard in the past two weeks. As the muscles in his weak leg grew stronger, Kip's times had improved steadily. He seemed to have a special aptitude for the stretching, slightly rolling motion of the backstroke.

While Kip stood waiting to get in the pool, Clarity thought about how he had changed through the winter months. He looked a lot older. The scar was still there on his thigh, but it had faded and was not especially noticeable now. His slender body was tough and lean rather than skinny. And he didn't look scared.

The Salamanders were on their feet as Kip's heat pulled for the end of the pool on their second and last lap. Kip and two other boys were far ahead of the others and matching each other, stroke for stroke.

"Gut it in, Kipper," Clarity screamed.

"Go, Moore!" yelled Brian, and even Dave O'Fallon, who was usually too busy playing cards to watch any of the races, was cheering.

In the end it was a matter of inches. The long-armed boy in the next lane touched in first, and Kip was second.

"You looked terrific," Clarity told him as he crawled out of the pool. "There's only two more heats. Maybe you qualified for the finals!"

"No chance," Kip said, but he couldn't help grinning, and his bue eyes sparkled with excitement.

In the state meet the eight swimmers whose times were fastest in each event swam again in a final race to determine the winners. These final races were held late in the afternoon on each of the two days. There was no way to tell who had made the finals until all heats were over and the times had been compared. Then the results were posted on the wall near the refreshment stand at the back of the room.

Clarity haunted the area as the meet moved on through the backstroke events for older swimmers. Melissa had an

excellent time in the girls ten-and-under backstroke and was almost sure of a place in the finals. She joined Clarity in prowling back and forth in front of the blank wall.

At last Stanley Boyd brought the first result sheet and taped it up with maddening slowness. Dozens of swimmers pushed close to see.

"You made it, Meliss!" Clarity whooped, peering at the list over someone's shoulder. "You're in the finals. You were fourth in the prelims . . ."

Then she saw Kip's name on the boys' event. He'd placed ninth, missing the finals by just a tenth of a second.

Butterfly came next. After getting her entry card, Clarity moved along the side of the pool with the others in her heat, watching the first races and getting more tense every

minute.

When they got to the benches behind the starting blocks and there was only one more heat to go, Clarity found that she'd been placed beside Wendy Whalen. Wendy would swim in lane three, and Clarity in lane four.

"Hot in here, isn't it?" Clarity asked her. "My uncle in Philadelphia built a sauna in his garage, and I *know* I never felt any more steamed in there than I do today."

Wendy said nothing at all. She glanced at Clarity and then turned back to the pool, ignoring her completely.

OK, High and Mighty Champion Swimmer, Clarity thought. Don't mind me. I'm not even here.

The more she thought about Wendy's snub, the angrier she got. She even forgot to be nervous about the race. She would show Wendy Whalen that there was someone in lane four.

When they were called to the starting blocks, Clarity took off her glasses and placed them carefully at the back of the block. The faces along the sides of the pool and the multi-colored flags above it all blurred out of focus. She concentrated on the blue-green water below.

Her dive felt good, and she came up in the undulating rhythm of the butterfly without having to think about her feet, her arms or her breathing. When her head was under water she watched the lines along the bottom of the pool to keep herself straight. Her mind was empty; for those few moments she was not even a person—just a swimmer.

At the end of the first lap she whacked both hands on the side. You could be disqualified for a one-handed touch in butterfly. Her feet whipped around and shoved her in the opposite direction, and at that moment she saw Wendy.

The Granite swimmer was only about half a body length ahead of her.

It was too soon to start breathing every other stroke, but Clarity did it anyway. Every time her head came up she expected to see the end of the pool. Her kick was getting weaker, and she was swallowing water. She looked at the next lane and saw only a splash. Vaguely, she heard screaming. Then she saw the end and slammed into the timer bar.

Wendy Whalen was already there. She reached across the lane rope and grabbed Clarity's hand. "Nice race," she said. At least she sounded hoarse and out of breath.

"Clare, you were second!" Melissa leaned over and pulled Clarity up and out of the pool.

"That's quite a time," Joe said, pointing to the lighted scoreboard on the wall. "Forty-one seconds. Only, you should have saved something for the finals."

"I wanted to beat Wendy. What was her time?" Clarity peered at the scoreboard, then remembered to get her glasses from the back of the starting block and looked again. "Wow, thirty-nine."

"And she wasn't pushing as hard as you were." Joe patted her shoulder. "Good race anyway. You're sure to be in the finals."

Clarity got hungrier and hungrier as the afternoon dragged on. She munched graham crackers and drank pop, but that didn't help very much. Her preliminary butterfly race had come shortly after noon, so she hadn't been able to eat lunch, and then she'd stayed by the pool to watch Joe place second in his butterfly event. Suddenly, at about four in the afternoon, she realized she was famished.

"I'm going to get a snack," she told Melissa, who was busy rebraiding June's hair for her.

"You can't eat now," Melissa said. "The finals will start pretty soon."

"Just something little." Clarity edged away, checking the amount of change left in her billfold. "They won't get around to butterfly for awhile. Anyway, I need some energy or I'll drown halfway down the pool."

She intended to have another snow cone, or at most a candy bar. It was the smell of the hot dogs that got to her as she waited in line. They came with fresh bakery buns, and an assortment of ketchup, mustard, pickle relish and onions. Clarity put everything on her hot dog, bought a bag of potato chips to go with it, and then decided she had to have soda pop to wash it down.

The food tasted wonderful. She ate it in a corner of the room, where she didn't think Joe was likely to spot her. He didn't like them eating before a race—but then everyone was different, Clarity told herself. Some people couldn't swim on a full stomach. She'd been doing it for years, ever since she'd learned to swim back home in the YWCA pool.

Clarity got back to the poolside in time to see Melissa place fifth in the backstroke finals. It was the first time a Silver Gulch swimmer had won a ribbon in a state championship meet.

The finals went quickly, since there was only one heat in each event. The older backstrokers were still in the pool when Clarity was called for the butterfly final.

And then the hot dog, potato chips and soda pop seemed to congeal into a rocklike object in the pit of Clarity's stomach. She felt like some kind of robot on a television commercial, with little men pounding her insides with hammers.

"Ugh, I think I made a big mistake," she mumbled to herself as they moved into position behind the starting blocks. Wendy Whalen was in the next lane again, but gave no sign that she'd heard. Clarity put her glasses on the block and bent over to wait for the starting gun.

This time nothing felt quite right. Her dive was too flat, and her arms and legs refused to get into the proper synchronization. Her shoulders ached from the effort she'd made in the preliminary race. On the last lap she forgot to watch the lines on the bottom and brushed the lane rope. Her stomach hurt the whole time.

When Clarity hit the timer bar Wendy was already climbing out in the next lane, her first-place medal assured. Two other girls had touched in already, and the other four surged in just behind Clarity. She'd taken fourth.

"Forty-three seconds, this time," Joe told her as he helped

her out of the pool. "Did you run out of gas?"

"Yeah, I guess so. Just didn't feel right. I'm surprised it wasn't slower than that."

"Well, fourth in the state isn't too bad, little sister. Congratulations."

The other Salamanders crowded around. They were proud, and it should have felt good, but Clarity knew she hadn't done her best this time. Her shoulders slumped as she walked away from the pool, and her stomach was still hurting.

"Hey, Moore!" Clarity turned and saw Wendy coming up behind her. "I thought you were the one I'd have to beat in the finals."

She didn't seem to be crowing. Clarity choked back an angry response and said, "I was tired. Anyway—I guess I ate too much just before the race." That sounds like a bunch of excuses, she told herself.

But Wendy grinned and nodded. "I did that once. I thought there was going to be an hour break before this race, and I ate a submarine sandwich. *I* felt like a submarine when I got in the water—with a broken-down engine. Why are you looking at me so funny?"

"Huh? Oh, I just wondered how come you're being friendly. I mean, I tried to talk to you before the prelim, and you didn't even answer."

"Didn't I? Well, I never talk to anybody right before a race. I get really nervous, and when I'm trying to get psyched up I don't even hear what people say to me."

"That's strange. When I'm nervous I talk a blue streak. Eat a ton, too," Clarity groaned.

"Bet you won't do that again, though." Wendy smiled and waved. "See you."

"Right." Clarity watched her go, feeling better about the whole day.

Sunday began with a poolside, nondenominational church service. Then the second day's events got under way.

It took hours to go through the freestyle events because so many swimmers were entered and there were nine or ten heats in every race. Neither Clarity nor Melissa came close to making the finals in freestyle, but June O'Fallon beat her best time by six seconds and her name was in the list of finalists. Joe also made the freestyle finals, as did Ted Beecher in the breaststroke. June finished eighth, Joe third, and Ted seventh. When all the individual events were over, Silver Gulch had earned a total of five ribbons.

"Not bad, for a team that didn't even exist last year," Mr. Moore said as the family gathered beside the bleachers for a moment.

"Yeah," Kip said, "especially since old Clare just sort of made the whole thing up."

"Was it such a bad idea?" she asked him. "You almost won a ribbon yourself . . ." Kip looked so downcast at that that she wished she hadn't mentioned his ninth place finish.

"No," Clarity said, "there's still the medley relay. We've got one of the best times in the program. And with Meliss placing in backstroke, June in free and me in 'fly, we should have a good chance for a ribbon or medal. Maybe even first!"

Backstroke came first in the medley relay, so Melissa stood behind the block as they waited for the race to begin. Cheryl Stein was behind her, tucking her long black hair into her swimming cap. Butterfly would be third, following Cheryl's breaststroke, so Clarity was next in line. At the end of Silver Gulch's team in lane four was June, their freestyler.

One other heat had already swum, but all the top teams were in this group of eight. The Granite team was two lanes down in two, with Wendy lined up to go against Clarity in butterfly. The team in lane three was from Riverside, a city in eastern South Dakota. They had the girl who won the gold medal in the individual freestyle competition.

"Remember not to take off until you see the swimmer before you touch in," Joe told the four Salamanders. "It doesn't matter how well you swim if you DQ; you're out of the race, and the whole team with you. Want me to take your glasses, Clare?"

"No, I want to see the beginning of the race. I'll put 'em on the block just before I dive."

"Don't forget . . ."

"I know, I know."

Melissa stayed with the leaders from Granite and Riverside on the first lap of backstroke. She turned perfectly and flipped back with such force that she actually pulled ahead of them, and was first by a second or so when Cheryl took off.

Cheryl's dive was as good as Melissa's turn. Clarity mentally thanked Joe for the hours he'd spent working with them on the racing dive as she watched Cheryl pull even farther ahead down her first lap. The Granite breast stroker hesitated a shade too long and then dove too deep, and Riverside's girl was just not particularly fast. Cheryl turned well and pulled steadily back down the pool, her head bobbing up and down as she breathed.

Clarity put her glasses at the back of the block and waited, her body curved and poised to dive. She watched

Cheryl's white cap, now a full length ahead of the swimmer in the next lane. Then she saw Cheryl's hands hit the bar, and dove.

Dimly aware of yelling and cheering when she came up to breathe, Clarity concentrated on holding straight and using every muscle in her body to move through the water. She felt loose, and good. The wall loomed ahead before she really expected it. She touched, tucked her head into the turn and kicked back strongly against the wall.

Several times she wanted to look over into the other lanes to see whether she was holding the lead, but Joe had warned her that she could waste a precious second or two doing that. With no idea at all of her position relative to the others, she used her last ounce of energy and emptied her lungs of air as she surged into the wall at the shallow end of the pool.

The room echoed with screaming. Clarity looked back and saw June splashing down the lane with a lead of several yards over the Granite swimmer and even more over the girl from Riverside. The other freestylers were not even in the water yet, but still waited on their blocks for the end of the butterfly laps.

"You held it, Clare!" Melissa yelled, reaching for her hand and pulling her out. "Whalen couldn't quite catch you. Now if June can just hang on . . ."

The uproar was fantastic. Swimmers, parents and coaches were on their feet, straining to see the result of the relay. A tall lane judge stood in front of Clarity, and after trying to see around him for a few second she climbed back onto the starting block for a better view and kicked her glasses into the water.

Clarity saw them fall into the churning, bluegreen stuff. After glancing down the lane to be sure the swimmers were still at the other end just making their turns, she went in after the glasses.

She grabbed them before they hit bottom and pulled back out of the pool at once. Then she put them on, wet as they were, and watched June fight to hold a slender lead over the Granite girl. From about midpool June breathed only every four strokes, and she did the last quarter of her lap without taking her head out of the water at all. She hit the timer bar first, just ahead of the Granite freestyler and not more than a second or two before the girl from Riverside, who had gained on both of them during the fifty meters.

"We won!" Cheryl screamed.

"Gold medals!" yelled Melissa, helping June out of the pool. The four of them jumped up and down, hugged each other, and accepted congratulations of their teammates and other people who crowded around them. Clarity's delighted grin faded as she watched Joe and Mr. Boyd pushing toward them, looking glum.

"What's wrong?" she asked Joe.

"You DQ'd, Clare," he told her.

"No, I'm sure I didn't dive until after Cheryl touched . . ."

"It's not that," Mr. Boyd said. The sympathetic look on his face brought Clarity's sinking spirits even lower. "You got in the pool during the race. That's against the rules. I'm afraid we have to give first place to Granite and disqualify you girls from Silver Gulch. I'm sorry."

9

Clarity looked around at Melissa, June and Cheryl. Her eyes burned, and the offending glasses felt huge on her face.

"I didn't think . . ." she croaked.

"I know, Clare," Joe said quickly. "And I never thought to tell you about that rule. I'm not sure I remembered it myself. Just didn't think it would come up, I guess."

"But she didn't interfere with the race," June protested to Mr. Boyd. "I was in that lane and I never even knew she got in the water. We were 'way down at the other end."

"I'm afraid that doesn't make any difference," Mr. Boyd said. "No one can get in the water in the course of an event except the entrants. We had to disqualify your team."

All the Silver Gulch swimmers had run up to congratulate the girls and were now realizing what had happened. For a minute nobody said anything. Clarity waited for them to start chewing her out. She knew they couldn't get any madder than she was at herself.

It was Dave O'Fallon, of all people, who stepped up

suddenly and punched Clarity's shoulder lightly. "Don't worry about it, Moore," he said.

"Yeah, Clare, you didn't know." Melissa managed a smile. "Maybe we should take up a collection to get you some contact lenses."

"Oh, no," Brian groaned. "Can you imagine looking for one of *those* in that water? Maybe we could get her a seeing-eye salamander."

"Go ahead, make jokes," Clarity said. "But I lost it for all of us . . . four gold medals. I wish they could just disqualify *me*."

June shrugged. "So do I, Clare. But it doesn't work that way, so we might just as well forget it."

"We know we won," Cheryl said. "We'll get those medals next year. Did you see our time? Two minutes fifty-eight seconds. That's the first time we ever beat three minutes. If we did it once, we can do it again."

Nothing could really make Clarity feel better, but behind her misery was a faint surprise at the way the Salamanders were trying to spare her feelings. A few months ago she hadn't even known any of them, except Melissa, Kip and Joe. Now they all seemed like old friends, or even a family. She'd have to think about it later. Right now she wanted to take off her glasses, break off both bows and throw them against the wall.

It seemed strange not to get up at dawn and go to early-morning swim team practice the next day. Clarity had washed her hair the night before, and now it was soft and dry instead of being damp or stiff with chlorine. She'd slept until seven and had a hot breakfast at home, and the world did not look quite so bleak as it had after the meet.

"After all," Melissa reminded her at lunch, "we won five ribbons. Nobody was laughing at us; they knew we had a real swim team. Remember that first meet, when we could hardly get down the pool?"

June cracked a hard-boiled egg on her head and peeled it into her napkin. "Yeah," she said, "and we didn't even have team suits, or anything. We were last in just about every event."

"Your brother could hardly walk, let alone swim," Melissa said as Kip and Dave raced through the lunchroom on their way to their daily noon soccer game. "Look at him now; he barely limps at all."

"I just wish he'd won a ribbon," Clarity said. "It's hard to come in ninth, especially when you like to win as much as Kip does."

As they were finishing that last few bites of lunch, Wendy Whalen walked up to their table and sat on the bench beside Clarity.

"Tough about that medley relay," she said. "I didn't know about that rule, either. You should have won it."

"Uh, thanks," said Clarity.

"Some of us were talking to our coach after the meet last night, and we had an idea. Why don't you kids from Silver Gulch join the Granite Swim Club? I mean, we could combine the two teams. You don't have enough swimmers to win any meets, and you've got those rotten practice hours."

"We're through with that until next fall," June told her.

"OK, but if any of you want to compete this summer you could swim for us, and then next fall we'd put the two clubs together. We go on a lot of out-of-town trips, and we have a big party every few months. Saturdays we have movies after practice . . ."

"Sounds like fun," Clarity said, "but what do you want with us? I mean, I thought your team was too big already. They wouldn't even let us try out last fall."

Wendy brushed a piece of hair back behind her ear. "Simple. You took three or four ribbons in the meet, right?"

"Five," said June.

"OK. Riverside won the meet, like they do every year. We came in second, only ten points behind them. Let's see, you get nine points for a first place, seven for second, six for third, five for fourth and so on. If we'd had your score too, we'd probably have won. Especially if we'd had a couple of your swimmers on our relay teams." Wendy stood up as the bell rang marking the end of lunch period. "Talk it over, and let us know what you think."

Joe called a meeting of the Silver Gulch swimmers and their parents at the motel the following Friday night. The kids sat around on the floor of the small living room, munching popcorn from large bowls Peg Moore had placed around the room. The adults occupied the chairs and the one long sofa, drinking coffee and looking around at Mrs. Moore's wildly abstract paintings.

Clarity explained the offer as Wendy had told her about it.

"We'd all be able to work with a real coach," Joe said. "Mrs. Marx has a lot of experience. She knows what she's doing."

"I don't see anything wrong with the coaching they've had," Mr. Kelly said. "You've done pretty well in just a

year. Of course, I don't know much about it, but I know
my boys have improved a great deal."

Joe shook his head. "Remember, we started practically
from scratch. I could teach the basic strokes and turns, but
that's about all I know. And it's hard to coach and swim on
the team, too."

"They got a lot of individual help this way, though," Mrs.
Stein pointed out. "With Granite each swimmer is one of,
what, ninety or so?"

"Yeah, that way we might get away with something once
in awhile," Cheryl said, turning her mother's comment
around. "Joe always sees every little mistake."

"I like those sweatshirts they have," said June. "They
even put your name on the back."

"We'd get to take more trips," Dave said. "One of the
guys on the Granite team told me that they went to a meet
in Canada once."

"Who goes on the trips, though?" asked Clarity. "Not
everybody; just the best swimmers."

Kip nodded. "That might be you, June, Melissa, Ken,
Ted and Joe. The rest of us would probably be on their 'B'
team, or maybe even the 'C' team. We'd go to meets like
the one at Lewisburg."

The parents began talking about costs of the Granite
team as compared to the expenses of financing the Silver
Gulch team. Clarity looked around the room, not really
listening. She saw Patty Allison tossing popcorn into her
mouth, kernel by kernel; Brad Kelly, too heavy and lazy
to be a top swimmer, but always ready with a good-natured
joke; Dave O'Fallon, the goof-off who could drive you crazy
but who was never really mean; and the others . . . Clarity

tried to imagine them all as part of the Granite Swim Club. Mrs. Marx would probably kick Dave out. There were a dozen better swimmers in Brad's age group, and Patty had to be coaxed into trying anything new. Kip might work himself onto the 'A' team, but Brian never could.

"I think we ought to keep the Salamanders together," Clarity said suddenly.

The discussion of finances stopped, and everyone turned to look at her. She hadn't realized that she'd spoken so loudly. "I mean, we've had fun this year. It wouldn't be the same if the Granite team just sort of swallowed us up," she finished lamely.

"But we're really too small to amount to much as a team, aren't we?" asked Mike Kelly.

"Who cares?" Clarity threw back at him. "So we can't win meets with only a dozen kids. We can each do the best we can, and have a lot of fun and maybe win some ribbons. We've got team suits, even a bus. I vote we stay the way we are."

Joe looked uncertain, and Clarity sensed that he wanted to agree with her but was afraid to admit it. People might think he just wanted to go on being the coach. "There are other things we can't do with such a small team," he said. "Like hosting a meet, for instance. We can't do it without a pool."

Everyone was quiet for a moment, and then Kip spoke. "I used to go in for all kinds of sports back in Philadelphia," he said. "Touch football, baseball, midget basketball, everything. You'd show up for the first practice and there'd be three hundred other guys on this big field. Somebody'd divide you up into teams, and you'd get this big schedule and play on a team with some kids and then there'd be another season and another sport and you'd never see most of 'em again. It was fun, and they had great uniforms and equipment and stuff, but—well, the swim team is different. Like Clare said, we know each other. It doesn't matter how good you are as long as you work out and do your best. I'd rather keep the Salamanders, too."

They took a vote, but it wasn't really necessary. Everyone in the room agreed at last that Silver Gulch should keep its swim team.

As Mr. Moore refilled the adults' coffee cups, Patty twisted on the piano bench to look out the window at the moonlit motel yard and the empty swimming pool. "How come we couldn't have a meet in that?" she asked.

"Too small, tadpole," Joe told her. "It's only fifteen yards long. Has to be at least twenty-five yards."

"Why?"

"Because all the races are measured in multiples of twenty-five yards or twenty-five meters."

"Wait a minute!" Clarity jumped up, spilling the last popcorn crumbs from the bowl that had been balanced in her lap. "Why couldn't we have a meet here? A mini-meet! Instead of the regular races we could have all sorts of crazy events, something different, just for fun. Like an underwater event, for instance. Or a relay where you balance something on your head."

"Diving for rocks," Ken Kelly suggested.

"One lap, feet first," said Ted Beecher.

"Wait a minute," Joe yelled as the ideas came faster and faster. "The AAU wouldn't let us give awards for that kind of thing . . ."

"I could make special ribbons," Peg Moore volunteered.

"And instead of regular entry fees for each event," said Melissa, "we could just charge each team ten dollars or something for the whole day. We could still have a refreshment stand and make money that way."

"How about a race for the parents?" asked Mr. O'Fallon. "I used to be a pretty fair swimmer myself."

"We could call it the First Annual Silver Gulch Salamanders Swim Carnival and Mini-Meet," Clarity said. "I can just see the fancy invitations my mother will draw for us."

"We'd still have to get the AAU to approve it," Joe told them. "Maybe they'd let us do it before the regular summer swimming season starts . . ."

". . . and the tourist season," added Leo Moore.

". . . and before I have to get my work ready for the July art festival," said Mrs. Moore, "if I'm going to draw these fantastic invitations and make the ribbons, too."

"I could be in charge of the refreshment stand," offered Mrs. Stein.

"And I'll shoot the starting gun," said Dave. " 'Judges and timers ready, swimmers take your marks—pow!' "

10

The Silver Gulch Motel looked fantastic in the early morning light—like a miniature circus had been set down in the mountain gulch by some magician. Bright flags waved above the pool. Folding chairs and benches had been set up all around it. Farther back in the yard, six parachutes had been staked out like tents, each one a different color and design. The refreshment stand, made of folding tables covered with worn-out motel sheets that Peg Moore had tie-died, stood near the office. Across the office itself hung a huge banner which said: "Welcome to the First Annual Silver Gulch Swim Carnival and Mini-Meet."

"We'll make a *fortune* today," Clarity said as she helped Kip and Joe set up the last of the folding chairs beside the pool. "Ten dollars a team, that's sixty dollars right there, plus the profits from the refreshment stand and a quarter for each program. We can afford to have a big party for the team some time this summer."

"This *is* a big party," Joe told her. "Whatever money we

make should go for a good stopwatch, and fixing up the bus."

"How about team sweatshirts like Granite has?" asked Kip.

"Well, I guess the whole team will have to decide about that later, after we see how much we make." Joe heaved the large table for the officials into position. "At least it's a nice day. It took all afternoon yesterday for Dad and me to get those parachutes up. I could just see a windstorm today blowing 'em all down again."

"They look great," Clarity said. "I'm glad Dad saw them in that army surplus store when he went back East last month. This way each team has a shady place to sit when they're not swimming, and there's no way you could get all those kids in our pool at once!"

"Speaking of that trip Dad made," said Kip, "I sure thought we'd be moving back East for awhile there."

"Yeah, the company really seemed to want him back." Clarity looked at the mountains just taking shape against the early-morning blue of the sky. They were like old friends now. At first the quiet had bothered her, but she'd learned to hear the different sounds of the gulch—the wind in the trees, the noises made by insects and animals and people. She turned to Kip. "Were you disappointed when he and Mom decided to stay here?"

Kip shrugged in his casual way. "I still miss the kids back there and some of the stuff we used to do. But I guess I like it here, too."

"Come on and eat breakfast," Mr. Moore yelled from a window of the house. "We'll finish setting up later. Blueberry pancakes!"

Nearly a hundred and fifty swimmers were there by ten o'clock, when the meet was to sart. Granite had the largest delegation of thirty-six. With coaches, parents, and a few motel guests milling around and adding to the confusion, the yard was mobbed.

Clarity was entered in the first event, a relay in which each swimmer had to have his feet bound with a piece of inner tube like those used in practices. The entrants would have to swim a length of the pool, then take off the band and pass it to the next member of the relay team.

Stanley Boyd had agreed to come to Silver Gulch and serve as starter for the meet. He smiled at Clarity, who was sitting beside him waiting for the boys' division of the event to begin. "Quite an idea you Salamanders had, putting on a meet like this in a motel pool," he said.

"This race was my idea," Clarity told him. "Remember when you showed Joe about those black bands for learning butterfly, and I had to wear one for a whole week?"

"Yes, I do. You learned to keep your feet together doing the dolphin kick, didn't you?"

"I sure did."

Just behind Clarity, June, Melissa and Cheryl were the girls from Granite. "I don't see how we're all going to swim in that oversized bathtub." one of them said.

Clarity heard Wendy Whalen reply, "Oh, quit griping. It'll be fun."

As the day went by it was amazing to see how excited and competitive the swimmers could get over contests that had no official status, no exact times or team scores or medals at stake. No one was tense or scared as they often were at a "real" meet, but there was just as much cheering for teammates and just as much effort to win each event.

The "Hobbled Relay" was followed by a sidestroke race, a "Feet First" event and a water polo tournament. There was a half hour break for lunch, while the refreshment stand was swamped with customers. Then came the "Senior Swimmers" events.

The swim teams deserted their parachutes and crowded around the pool as the parents lined up for the individual contests in freestyle, breast stroke and back stroke. Clarity had wanted to include butterfly as well, but none of them knew how to do it.

The Salamanders bunched together and screamed, "Go, Mrs. Moore!" as the women's freestyle event began. A lady from Lewisburg won it, but Peg Moore finished a strong second. Later, Mr. O'Fallon took first in the men's backstroke.

After the "Seniors" were through it was time for the underwater races. Boys and girls in each age group would see who could do the most laps without coming up for air. Kip was in the last heat of the boys' ten-and-under-category, and Clarity shoved close to the pool to watch him.

The record to this point was two laps, or thirty yards. All six of the boys in this last heat made the first lap easily; two of them came up for air on the way back. Kip and another boy flipped after the second lap and started back on a third. Clarity cheered wildly, though she knew Kip couldn't possibly hear her. Both of the boys rose toward the surface as their air ran out. Then halfway down the pool the other boy's head came up, and just a few seconds later Kip also thrust up through the water, gasping like a beached fish.

"First place!" Clarity announced, and as Kip dragged himself out of the pool she saw him grin as though he'd just won a gold medal at the state meet.

It was late in the afternoon when Mrs. Moore's ribbons were handed out by Mr. Boyd at an awards ceremony on the lawn beside the pool. Each ribbon was a miniature work of art, with psychedelic designs or tiny paintings of Black Hills scenes. Kip's blue ribbon had a pine tree on it like the one he'd been climbing when he hurt his leg.

After all the ribbons had been distributed, Mr. Boyd asked Joe to come forward to make a special presentation.

"As you all know, this was the first season for the Silver Gulch Salamanders swim team," he said. "Today we've got a special award for the person who thought up the idea and really got the team together. She's sort of a nut sometimes, but we're stuck with her. Clarity Jean, come up here."

Clarity wriggled through the crowd to the place where Joe stood. She brushed her wet hair back out of her eyes and looked around nervously. Kip came forward, his first place ribbon for the underwater swim still in one hand and the other hand behind his back.

"We could have got you a loving cup or something dumb like that," Kip said, "but instead we decided to give you an award you really *need*. So the rest of us got together at Kelly's and made you this."

Kip handed her a tooled-leather glasses case, with "Clarity Moore" on one side and a picture of a salamander on the other. A pair of long leather thongs were laced through the top of it. "With these," Kip said, "you can tie the case to the starting block or hang it from the ceiling— anything you want."

"Thanks." Clarity took the case and slipped her glasses

into it. "I promise never to kick them into the pool again." And she meant that promise. The team had come to mean too much to her. She was determined never to spoil their chances in a future meet.

Mrs. Stein got the older boys to help pass out little cartons of ice cream to all the swimmers at the meet. Clarity, Melissa and June sat around the base of the big elm tree to eat theirs.

"Hey, when did you make this, anyway?" Clarity asked, holding up the glasses case.

"Those two days when you had to stay in Granite and go to the dentist after school," Melissa told her. "Ken and Brad Kelly did the cutting and stuff, but we all helped to decide what it should look like."

June pointed to the picture on the back of the case. "I found a salamander in our encyclopedia," she said. "It was my idea to put that on."

"Looks kind of like a lizard, doesn't it?" said Clarity.

"It can live just about anyplace," June said, "land or water. And even if you cut off its leg, it could grow another one."

"Pretty tricky beast." Clarity looked around at her teammates, at Kip showing his ribbon to Dave, at the swimmers from the other towns gathering their belongings and heading for the cars parked along the road, at the tree-fringed hills and the dimming sky above. "But can it swim?"

"If it has to," said June.

NANCY VEGLAHN grew up in Sioux City, Iowa, and graduated from Morningside College there. While her husband, Don, was studying at Yale Divinity School, the Veglahns lived in Connecticut, the setting of her earlier Weekly Reader Children's Book Club title, THE VANDALS OF TREASON HOUSE. Mrs. Veglahn now lives in Brookings, South Dakota, with her husband and two children. She is an active golfer, a member of the League of Women Voters, a reader of American history, and a busy writer. SWIMMERS, TAKE YOUR MARKS! is her ninth book for young readers.